# Demon Awaken

Ash Miller

Michael Terence
Publishing

First published in paperback by
Michael Terence Publishing in 2020
www.mtp.agency



ISBN 9781800940680

*This book is dedicated to my mum, Peggy Eaton,*
*who we lost in 2020.*

*Following in footsteps…*

# One

Mike Dean had become aware that something wasn't right. That sensation had been growing over a period of days, becoming stronger by the moment. It was a gut feeling, one that was bugging him, not letting him have any peace. The biggest problem was that he couldn't put his finger on exactly what was wrong, but he was certain that it was there. It was hanging on, nagging at the back of his mind, like the remains of a whiskey hangover. Mike had become more convinced that something wasn't right as time passed. The one thing that he was certain of was that whatever was going on, it wasn't normal.

Events took a turn for the worse in the overgrown and desolate graveyard of an old Swedish church. Mike had followed Rick Fischer into the cemetery, determined to work out what was going on. The site that he had found himself in was old and at first glance appeared largely derelict. All the brickwork of the walls was crumbling and weather-worn, the scattered gargoyles looked precariously balanced and about to fall. From a distance, Mike couldn't get the idea out of his mind that the bell tower might collapse at any moment, if there was a stiff gust of wind. That strange excursion had come as a break from the normal tour routine for Mike. At the time he was working for a rock band called The Demon Eaters.

The Demon Eaters were two weeks into their first full European tour, taking in a series of small to medium size venues. The dates were proving to be successful, which was a relief to the band. They were all aware that there was a long road ahead, before they could take the rock world by storm. After what had been a slow start, the tour had now grown some momentum and had stepped up a gear. Now that the word was out, far larger crowds were turning up regularly.

It was when they rolled into the third week of the tour that Mike Dean first noticed Rick Fischer's unusual behaviour. Straight away, he suspected that he was up to something. There was a feeling that didn't sit right about his actions. The tour manager, was unquestionably acting in a suspicious way. Mike hadn't noticed it until that moment, but once he spotted it, it was unmistakable to him. Rick was sliding off regularly, but he did it when he was certain that no one was watching him. Of course, there was nothing unusual in wanting to run away from the day-to-day routine. He would often look for space himself, a chance to escape the rest of the company for a brief period. The tour routine could become claustrophobic after a few weeks. Finding some time for yourself would be a vital way of keeping your head together.

The daily routine meant living for weeks on end, cocooned in the cramped confines of a tour coach. It was something that could be hard for some people to handle. As they travelled from town to town, city to city, the mundane repetition could become oppressive and difficult to deal with. Everyone needed to find a way of grabbing a little personal time and space. It was a way of coming to grips with things mentally. Some people did it by locking themselves away or going off for regular long walks. It was all a natural part of the touring regime, they would all find their own modes of survival. The reason that Mike's attention had become aroused was the way that Rick Fischer acted in secret. It was as if he didn't want to run the risk of someone following him, seeing what he was up to.

Once his attention had sparked, Mike Dean was well aware that he wouldn't be able to help himself. He now wanted to discover what it was that Rick Fisher was up to. At the end of the day, he expected to see that it was all innocent. He would find that Rick was off searching for souvenirs or something boring like that. Part of the problem was that Mike had to admit that he despised the man. He had met him for the first time at the start of the tour and the dislike had grown as the weeks passed. Despite that, he was sure that Rick's actions would all turn out to be innocuous in the end. Even with the idea in the back of his mind, he couldn't rid himself of the feeling that there was more to it. There was something about his level of secretiveness; it was odd and it didn't sit at all right with him.

Mike waited for a point when they had a couple of rest days, before their gig at Gothenburg's Trädgår'n Concert Hall. Early that first morning, he kept a tight watch on everything that was going on. He was certain that Rick would want to take advantage of the occasion and run off yet again. That night in Gothenburg had seen them staying in a slightly dingy but comfortable hotel. Mike forced himself to get up early, after the luxury of a proper bed, rather than his bunk on the tour bus. For the next hour he sat there on his own in the barely occupied breakfast room. He drank several cups of potent black coffee, the idea that he was wasting his time coming into his head once again. The bread rolls that he had eaten, adorned with tasteless cheese and layers of thin ham, did little to raise his mood. After the best part of an hour sitting there alone, Tac and Joey appeared. Surprised to see him up and about at such an early time, they joined him at his table.

Mike Dean had been working with Tac for several years, and he had become great friends with the flamboyant guitarist. The founding member of The Demon Eaters, Tac had formed the band to further develop his ideas. Mike had been Tac's guitar technician, while he had been playing in his two previous line-ups. That had included the monumental Gypsy Sioux, a group that would always live in Mike's mind as one that should have gone on to far greater success. They should have been superstars. Mike had been sure that the Gypsy Sioux were on the way to the big time from the first moment that he had heard them. The band fell apart in the end when the bass player died in a car crash, after a night out to celebrate the end of a tour.

Although Tac had always found it hard to deal with people, he became friendly with Mike from the moment that he first met him. They discovered that they had a lot in common and enjoyed each other's company. It was something that helped when you were out on the road. Over the years that they had been working together, their families had become close too. Their girlfriends had formed a small company, selling tour merchandise. When The Demon Eaters reached the stage where they were ready to head out on the road, Mike was the first person they brought in. Tac was well aware that he could trust him to do a professional job. He would also be able to act as a safety net for him. Over the years he had become a little bit like a counsellor, a crutch to lean on, when Tac was feeling vulnerable. It was a pit that Tac found himself falling into every now and then.

The Demon Eaters were the first line-up that Tac had put together himself. It was a project that he had been planning for years but his insecurities had managed to get in the way. The band was a vehicle for him to showcase both his own song writing and his guitar skills. He had enjoyed playing other people's material, but now it was the right time to take his career on to the next stage. For years Tac had been the lead guitarist in different line-ups, a few of them had been good, others not so.

He had always had the urge to try going it alone at some point, when he was able to pluck up the courage. Tac was a massive presence, one that could take any band up an extra level by having him on the stage with them. Once The Gypsy Sioux had imploded in such disastrous circumstances, he decided the time had come. At last he would do it his own way, instead of working with other people and playing their material.

Knowing what Tac was like, Mike Dean was certain that the band would be great, as soon as Tac told him about them. Even then it came as a surprise when he heard the direction that Tac had taken them in. The flashy glam rock feeling of the other line-ups that he had played in over the years had now disappeared. The Demon Eaters were a growling hard metal band with a powerful live sound and image to match. They were using heavy industrial beats to broaden the dynamics of their numbers, giving them a whole new dimension. That was something Tac had never shown any interest in before. Mike had no idea where that sound had come from. It was unlike any material that Tac had ever done in the past, but he was loving every minute of it.

From his first listen, in a dingy basement studio, Mike was aware that this was something exceptional. Despite the inadequate PA system, he could see that the resulting sound was going to be powerful. Tac had been working on the band for several months by that time, but he had told Mike little about what he was building. All he had done was to drop the odd hint, whenever they met up. During those long weeks, he had been honing the sound that he was after, forcing his guitar into new levels of intensity. By the time that Mike came in, the band had been in the studio for several months. He soon found that all the equipment was in need of a thorough service. Everything appeared to be on the verge of packing up.

Mike Dean loved the new sound from the first day that he had heard it in that gloomy basement. He was more than happy to join up as an integral part of the band's crew, when Tac asked him to. Since the Gypsy Sioux had ended, Mike had been out on several tours, with some up-and-coming groups. In that time there had been little that had grabbed him. Those bands were all great but there was nothing exceptional about them. Mike had always suspected that Tac had a darker side to him. Something hidden, lurking underneath all the glam make up and peacock showiness. Now he could dispense with his previous incarnations at last. He had even allowed his electric blue hair to grow out, during the time in the studio. It was now back to its long forgotten dark, near black colour, and hung across his shoulders in untidy waves. Mike was happy to see this other side coming out. With this line-up, Tac could be himself and go where he wanted to go, wherever that might end up being.

* * *

For several days, the tour routine rolled ever onward, and Mike Dean tried to keep patient. In time, he found the chance that he had been waiting for. It was his opportunity to follow Rick Fischer on one of his secretive jaunts. He had been certain that it would come around, and he had been expecting that moment to arrive. He was pouring yet another cup of rich black coffee, when he happened to look up and spotted Rick. Within an instant, he had darted out of the hotel's main entrance and into the street. There had been a single brief glance over his shoulder, as he reached the door. It appeared as if he wanted to check whether anyone was watching, then he was off. Although Rick was not running, he was in some hurry as he darted up the street.

Within moments of Rick Fischer's disappearance, Mike Dean was on his feet. He followed him out of the hotel, up the street and onto the now busy main Stampgatan. The early morning rush hour crowds made it easy for Mike to stay out of his vision. He wanted some space between them but without having to lag too far behind his quarry. The risk of discovery weighed against the idea of losing sight of him. It was lucky that the crowds were there, drifting around, when Mike saw Rick jump onto a passing tram. Luckily, he was close enough to be able to board the second carriage. Concealing himself amongst the press of other passengers, Mike kept vigilant. The tram pulled off into the busy morning traffic, crossing the river. Within a short space of time they were heading away from the centre of the city.

As he had no idea where they might be going, Mike Dean tried to keep an eye on Rick's movements. He was sitting a short distance away from him in the front carriage, looking relaxed and calm. Mike could see him through the crowd and didn't want to move any closer, wary about keeping out of his eyeline. If Rick was to turn around and look back, he wouldn't want to be in his vision. He had no idea how he would explain himself if Rick happened to notice him. He had run through several possible explanations but was well aware that they would all sound pathetic. Mike didn't want to have to use any of them, with that in mind, he kept his head down whenever Rick did turn around. Every now and then he glanced about, as if checking the street layout to be sure of where he was. Watching for any sign that he was going to jump off, Mike waited with bated breath.

They were on the outskirts of the city, when the inevitable happened. The crowds were far thinner than they had been in the centre, all adding to Mike Dean's sense of caution. He now tried to keep his distance from Rick, as far as it was possible to. He realised that his discovery would be inexplicable. There would be no argument about bumping into him by accident. It would be clear that he had been stalking him. Watching from the doorway of an antiques shop, Mike saw Rick stroll off ahead of him. He appeared to be in a hurry, as if he was late for an appointment he had to keep. A hundred yards up the road, he turned up a side street, disappearing from view for a few moments. Following in his footsteps, Mike reached the corner himself as rapidly as possible.

Hurrying off after his man, Mike Dean took the bend in the road in time to see Rick strolling up a tree-lined roadway. Negotiating the twists and turns, Mike made his way up the shallow hill. The trees that were growing every hundred yards along the quiet street helped him to stay concealed. He followed as closely as he was able to, without being spotted. When Rick came to a stop, he was outside an ancient church. The building sat inside a large walled graveyard, looking distressed and sorry for itself. By that time Mike was a few hundred yards behind, and he froze beside a builders' truck that was parked nearby. It was clear that Rick was aware of exactly where he was going. He entered through the old wooden, gothic looking, entranceway. There was one brief glance over his shoulder, before he strolled on. With a purpose, he followed the path that led along the left-hand side of the tired church building.

As he reached the corner, Rick Fischer turned around again. Standing there totally still beside the building, he took a few moments to roll a cigarette. For a time, he stared back at the scene that he had walked through. He was clearly studying the pathway, the perimeter and road beyond. Mike Dean watched from behind a high brick pier in the surrounding wall. He knew for sure that Rick was checking to make certain that no one was observing him. Once he was happy that he was alone, Rick dropped the cigarette and crushed it under his heel. Leaving the pathway behind, he made his way through the scattered gravestones. Making his way towards the northern edge of the churchyard, he hurried on.

Mike reached the cover of the church wall, where Rick had earlier stopped to look back. From there he could view what was going on without being noticed. He watched Rick drop down to his knees and start digging a hole near to the foot of the wall. Once it was deep enough for him, he pulled something out of his pocket and placed it into the opening. Glancing around for one final time, he added a thin black candle on top of the buried object and lit it. A few tense moments passed and it seemed as if he was praying, although who to, Mike couldn't guess. As he looked on, he caught sight of a strange dull light hanging in front of Rick. It was little more than a faint smudge of white against the northern wall. His first impression was that he was imagining it but then it shifted in the air, and he was certain that it was there. After a few moments of inactivity, Rick leapt back to his feet. Stamping his foot down on the candle, he put the flame out, grinding it into the damp earth at the same time.

Rick Fischer's assignment was now over, whatever that bizarre mission had been. He turned and made his way back through the graveyard, without a second look. Strolling past the church, he walked out of the gateway, not stopping for a minute. By that time Mike Dean had managed to hide himself behind a large marble obelisk. He had ducked down the moment that he realised Rick was heading back in his direction. Crouching there, his breath held, Mike kept as still as possible and watched him stroll off down the hill. As he disappeared amongst the trees lining road, Mike noticed that the faint smudge of white was following him, hanging in the air behind him. He couldn't help wondering what it could be, it wasn't something that he had ever seen before. Once Rick had left the graveyard, Mike looked across the scrubby grass. In the distance he could see the crumbling northern wall where Rick had been standing. That was where he had earlier performed what had appeared to be some sort of private ritual.

"What the hell was that all about?" Mike Dean asked, talking to no one other than himself as he clambered back to his feet, shaking his head in puzzlement.

Mike Dean knew that he would have to try to uncover the secret of what Rick Fischer had been up to. He walked across the damp ground towards the far wall taking as much care as possible. Avoiding the scattered gravestones, he tried to stick to the drier patches of grass. A few moments later, he found himself at the spot where Rick had been kneeling. He could still see a slight waft of thin grey smoke that was drifting in the light breeze. The cloud of smoke rose like a troubled spirit from out of the ground where the candle had been. As he drew closer to the spot where Rick had been standing, he found an uncomfortable sensation washing over him.

When he was a couple of feet away from the crumbling wall, he noticed a foul smell that was in the air. The unpleasant stench hung in the air like a dull weight. Threatening to turn his stomach, it assaulted his nostrils and grew in intensity as he moved closer. It was an acrid sweet aroma that drifted around in the lazy breeze. Mike couldn't shrug off idea that it was the result of rotting meat, or something that had decayed in the back of a fridge. As the distinct stench hit his senses, he took his handkerchief out of his pocket. Clamping it tight over his mouth and nose, he managed to find some relief from the smell.

Mike Dean reached the spot where Rick Fischer had been standing. Looking down, he saw something protruding from the ground. The flattened tip of the smoking candle, stuck out from the mound of earth. Rick's boot prints still showing in the damp soil that he had roughly stamped down. It had been a definite attempt at concealment. Having carried out the job in a rush, he had not executed it very well. Looking around him, Mike unconsciously copied what Rick had been doing beforehand. Making sure that there weren't any eyes on him, he dropped to his knees and pulled a damp clod of earth away from the hole.

Removing a black stub of candle wax, Mike Dean found a small, roughly textured square brick. The piece of brickwork lay a couple of inches below the surface, it was a deep red in colour and harsh and fragile to the touch, as if it would crumble if he squeezed it. Brushing away a layer of the dirt that had become stuck to the brick, he examined it closely. Mike found a strange symbol carved into the top surface. A little of the molten black wax from the candle had filled the hollow lines. The wax made the symbol stand out as if highlighted, looking like a stylised letter Y.

Mike Dean was unable to make any sense of the incident. The strange ritual that he had seen Rick Fischer performing was bizarre. Was this what he was doing every time he ran off, Mike couldn't shake off the question about what it could all mean, it stuck in his head and wouldn't let go. Kneeling there on the damp ground, he was aware of the dark patches growing on the knees of his jeans. Mike stared down at the carved brick, trying to decide what to do next. Mike had no idea what had played out before him, what he had been witness to. At that moment he became aware of the faint ring of voices from somewhere off in the distance. Clambering back to his feet, he glanced around to see if he could locate where the sound was coming from.

Covering the hole over once again, he stamped the soil back into place. He couldn't help judging that he had accomplishing the task far better than Rick had done. Trying to brush the clinging shreds of grass from his knees, he attempted to make himself look a little less grubby. There was nothing that he could do about the dark damp circles that stood out on his pale blue jeans. He hoped that they would dry out on his way back to the hotel. As he walked towards the pathway, he saw an elderly couple carrying a large bunch of flowers. Tears sparkled in their ageing eyes, as they passed him, heading into the graveyard.

The elderly couple continued on without as much as a second glance at Mike. As soon as they were out of sight, he took off in the opposite direction. He strode along the pathway, heading for the gateway in the perimeter wall. Within moments, he was off down the road and making the descent back towards the main tram route. Leaving the churchyard behind with its mysteries, he couldn't help running through all the unanswered questions in the back of his head. He soon reached the tram stop, close to the bottom of the hill. With some relief, he found that there was no sign of Rick Fischer. Mike had been half expecting to discover him waiting to catch the next tram into the city centre. He was well aware that he would have had some explaining to do if they had run across each other.

Mike Dean had a five-minute wait before the next tram arrived. After sitting there, lost in his own thoughts, he found himself coming towards the city centre. He watched the thriving streets of the busy city as they expanded around him. Drawing ever nearer to the stop closest to the hotel, he kept a sharp eye out for Rick. Mike had managed in his goal of trying to determine what Rick Fischer was up to. The problem now was that far more questions had sprung up than answers. What was the man up to, his behaviour now looked stranger than it had ever done in the past. What could it all mean, he asked himself. Was it some kind of harmless ritual, the whole outing rolled around in the back of his mind. It left him feeling edgy and a little nervous.

The following day, after a night lazing in the hotel's bar, life returned to normal. The resumption of the usual tour routine set in, as they moved on to the next gig on the schedule. They had an early morning load-in booked for that day. It had been Tac's idea, he wanted the band to work through some numbers that he hadn't been happy with in the set. The half-asleep local crew that had assembled for the load-in proved to be more of a hindrance than a help. In the end, after a couple of hours, they had set up all the band's equipment, they were now ready for their arrival. By late morning, following a rushed breakfast, Mike Dean was back at work in his corner of the backstage area. It wasn't long before he had surrounded himself with Tac's guitar racks. He set out to clean, restring and tune the instruments, one by one.

As Mike Dean was working, Rick Fischer walked round a curtain completely out of the blue. He barged straight into the case of equipment that Mike had set up. At the time Rick had been in the middle of an intense discussion on his phone. Focused on his call, he hadn't noticed that Mike was there, working away in the dark corner of the backstage area. Rick stopped the conversation that he was having in mid flow. Pressing the button to switch the phone off, he slid it back into his pocket all in one fluid movement. The whole way that Rick had acted reminded Mike of a sleight of hand magician that he had seen during a night out at a London club. Apologising for having nearly knocking the guitars over, Rick set off in the opposite direction. Darting across the stage, he jumped off into the auditorium.

The whole way that Rick had reacted to the possible collision was odd. Mike Dean had the distinct impression that the conversation hadn't finished. It appeared as if Rick didn't want to take the chance that someone might be eavesdropping on what he was saying. Mike's suspicions were now growing, they were building a momentum of their own. Considering everything that had happened on the previous day's trip to the graveyard, that wasn't surprising. After all the things that he had seen Rick Fischer doing, the whole incident stuck in the back of his mind. He couldn't help speculating about the man's motives and what he was hoping to achieve with his bricks and candles. Mike decided that from that point on, he would keep a closer eye on Rick Fischer's every move. Now he would be searching for any sign, any clue to what was going on.

# Two

"Somehow, I could sense her again today, that bitch.

"Oh, yeah, she was there alright. I'm certain she was.

"It was when I was out there in that bloody graveyard. That's when she came to me again.

"I could tell that she was there with me. Course, I couldn't see her, could I?

"I sensed her presence as I chanted the first part of the incantation. She timed that to perfection! It caused me to lose the flow of words for a moment, and believe me, they ain't that easy to remember at the best of times.

"Had to restart the whole chant, had to be sure that I was getting it right, that I hadn't fucked it up.

"Can't afford to make mistakes on something like that, now, can I?

"I've no idea who or what she is. Not sure where the idea of her being a woman came from. I ain't seen nothing to tell me that she's female. I can't even be sure that she's really there, whether I'm imagining the whole damned thing. Losing my mind!

"She only started bugging me once I set all this in motion properly, when I found the ritual that I was after. It was the one that would raise the beast, Baphomet. He's the one that can give me the power I want.

"I can't help thinking that she's a figment of my imagination. Am I going insane? I think not. Think I'm being quite logical about all this.

"This will all come to fruition, I will raise the beast. The world will fall before his hands. His power will be eternal and it will be me standing there beside him, on his right-hand side. No one's going to stop me now!

"This all started when I found those papers in the old man's loft, after he dropped dead. "I hadn't seen him for a few years. We'd never been close, not since I left the country, we hadn't spoken more than a couple of times. Odd forced and uncomfortable phone calls they was. Pretty meaningless to both of us.

"When I got the message that he'd passed away, I was out in Germany, as was often the case at that time. You see, I'm more at home out there, I can be myself instead of being expected to fit in.

"I rushed home, don't really know why I was in such a hurry. It was too late for me to do anything about it, he was already dead by that time, but I made it back for the funeral, just.

"There were a few other blokes there. All in their seventies and eighties, like him. He had few close friends, as far as I was aware, and had become a little bit of a recluse, from what I'd heard. He never got on with people, did my old man.

"I can understand that, suppose I can be like that at times. Ha! Must run in the fucking family that, mustn't it.

"Anyway, there were six of us there, can't say I recognised any of the others, although three of them came over to speak to me. They seemed to know who I was, that I was his son. It's possible they guessed, I was the youngest person there after all, suppose it was obvious, that.

"The chat I got from them was the normal funeral type chat.

Saying nothing, going nowhere. Pointless, boring and meaningless, why do people have to say anything at all?

"They all told me how sorry they was for my loss, but I couldn't truthfully say that I was feeling any loss. To be honest, he'd been a pain in the ass most of the time. Still, I put up with them, thanked them for coming and all that garbage. Seemed to make them happy, or maybe they was just humouring me?

"A couple of them was expecting some kinda wake or something but fuck that, I weren't planning nothing like that. Didn't want to spend any more time with them than I had to.

"It was a few days after the funeral, I discovered the truth about the old house in Brighton. The one sat right at the top of that bloody hill, looking out over the race course. It was now all mine. I'd only bleeding inherited it!

"I gotta admit that I didn't realise he owned it. For some reason I always believed that he rented it. Anyway, we never talked about matters like that, even when we was on speaking terms.

"I grew up in that damned house, travelled to school and back from there. Vaguely remember me mum trying to decorate it, way back in the past. It's one of the few memories I have of her. Course, she must have done most of the work herself, can't see him having helped. He wouldn't have been able to tell one end of a paint brush from the other.

"I found out about the house when I met up with the slimy git that was his solicitor. He informed me that there was an insurance policy and a savings account linked to his bank account. More than enough to sort out all the ridiculous funeral fees, he told me, with a smug grin. It would leave a reasonable amount behind, the solicitor explained.

"That came as a surprise, didn't expect to come away with anything. He seemed to be completely broke most of the time, always struggling to pay for anything.

"Well, the house at the top of Elm Grove now belonged to me, the solicitor told me. He also had a letter with my name printed on the envelope, marked 'private'. Said it had been entrusted to him to pass on when he died. Why the fuck do they use language like that, entrusted to him? Why not just say it had been given to him? Guess they want to make themselves sound important, using words that no one else would. Twats!

"Now, that letter intrigued me from the moment that I first opened it, sitting there in the solicitor's office. I could sense his beady eyes staring at me from across his desk, like a malignant rat, his smug face grinning at me.

"That letter opened boringly enough. The old man's handwriting was its usual untidy scrawl, making it hard to read at times. Wasn't saying anything that was worth saying. There was some stuff about mum, a bit telling me what I should be doing with my life, what I could become?

"At the top of the second page was something that read as some kinda warning. It didn't have that effect on me though, it acted like a fucking magnet. It grabbed my attention and drew me in. The letter told me that up in the loft of the house there was a suitcase and that I should dispose of it straight away?

"Don't attempt to open it, it warned me, don't try to look through the contents, it said. Burn the lot, suitcase and all, the letter said. No good will come from my going through it, the old man told me, I should destroy it all for the good of the world.

"Well, that all sounded over-the-top to me. Course, I knew he could be overdramatic at times, but it was the last line that grabbed me the most. It stated that if I didn't destroy the case, she would follow me everywhere. She would haunt me, the letter said, mysteriously.

"Well, who the fuck was 'she' supposed to be, I couldn't help wondering.

"I scanned through the letter twice, wanting to be sure of what I'd read. I thanked the solicitor and signed all the papers that he asked me to put my name to, there was loads of them! After shaking his greasy hand, he kinda put me in a position where I had to, I grabbed the keys to the house. He'd dropped them onto the desk in front of me, as soon as I could, I escaped his office.

"Course, all I wanted to do was discover what the old man had stashed away in the attic. There was no way that I was going to destroy it, like he asked, whatever it was.

"Sometimes, I can't help feeling that he'd done all this to deliberately draw me in. Set me up. That he understood me far better than I thought he did.

"If he'd asked me to follow all this through, would I have done it? No, course not.

"Somehow, I'm sure I would have laughed at him, taken it for the absurdity that it appeared to be. Pretty sure that I wouldn't have even looked for the damned case.

"No, I wouldn't have done any of this, if he'd asked me to. Telling me not to, telling me to destroy it, yeah, what better way to make sure that he hooked me?

"Damn clever, my old man. I've got to give him that, he was too damn clever.

"Thinking back, I could remember as a kid, him talking to me about black magic and stuff like that. He loved the subject, had all kinds a books and things about it. Bedtime reading, when he still used to read to me, when I was what, nine or ten, it was always supernatural stories. Ghost stories, the supernatural, anything weird and wonderful like that.

"Course, at the time I lapped it up. I loved all those scary tales, even when they kept me up half the night, searching under the bed for ghosties! Afraid to open the cupboard doors when the lights were out!

"My teachers at school? Well, course, they hated it all. Whenever I spoke about things like that, tried to put it in my homework, in my essays.

"It intrigued some of the other kids in my classes, they was interested when I had to read things out in front of them. Most of them looked at me as if I was some kind of oddity, and they kept their distance.

"Course, I could tell they were taking the piss behind me back. Talking about me all the time but I tried to ignore them, let them get on with it.

"Yeah, I didn't have too many friends at school, but I can't think why I'm telling you all this. Should get back to the subject, shouldn't I; my old man's suitcase.

"I climbed that damned hill to the old man's house, sorry, my house. It was about five o'clock that evening by the time I got up there. Elm Grove! I'd always hated Elm Grove, too bloody steep, hell of a walk that was. He had to live at the top, didn't he, couldn't be comfortable at the bottom of the hill. It was somewhere that he could look out over the whole city, course it never seemed to be that steep when I was a kid.

"I was pretty tired when I got up there. It'd been a stressful day. Don't like dealing with solicitors and people like that, at the best of times. At least it was all done and dusted now, I told myself. I could now get on with my life.

"I drank a cup of coffee and followed it with a large whiskey, found the bottle of Jack stashed away in a kitchen cupboard. Once I was feeling more comfortable, I made my way up the stairs. His bedroom would have to wait, I couldn't face having to deal with that. Course, what I wanted was the attic.

"Should have been easy that, shouldn't it? Could I find it? Could I fuck!

"No hatch in the ceiling that I could see. Had he been winding me up all the time, I wondered, had he been taking the piss.

"I tried to remember when I was a kid, when I still lived there. Could I recall an attic? No, nothing, no memory at all, it could have been a million years ago. Becoming frustrated by that time, I went outside into the street. I studied the roof from the front, walked round the back and looked again. Could I see any sign of an attic, no, there was nothing.

"By that time I was stumped, pissed off and frustrated.

"Slamming the door as I walked out, I made my way down to one of the local pubs that I could remember being okay. I needed a damned drink by that time and the whiskey had gone."

# Three

The Demon Eaters tour rolled on across Eastern Europe. The band taking their unique brand of rock'n'roll to the receptive audiences of Riga, Minsk and Kiev before travelling into Romania. They would next have the luxury of a day off when they reached Bucharest. In the country's capital city they would be performing at the Fire Club, deep in the old town. That was a gig they were all looking forward to, having heard great reports about the venue. That area of Eastern Europe was all new territory for Mike Dean. Other than a brief three-day holiday in Poland, several years earlier, he had spent no time there. He had never had the chance to travel there before, but it had long been an area that he had wanted to discover.

None of the tours that he had worked on in the past had covered that part of Eastern Europe. Those tours had all concentrated on the audiences throughout the UK and central Europe. Travelling to Eastern Europe had long been an area that he wanted to visit but the chance had never appeared. There had been one opportunity, a few years before, but he hadn't been able to afford the extra outlay for the trip. By the time that they arrived in Romania, the whole crew had become used to sleeping in their bunks. The countless miles rolling away through the night hours as they slept. They would wake up each morning in some new town, new country. For a few people it could be disorientating, trying to work out where they were when they woke up. Whatever happened, it wasn't long before they were ready for the day ahead, as they entered yet another venue.

It was one of the things Mike Dean always found slightly hard to adjust to, when he was out on a lengthy tour. The clandestine passing of landmarks while he slept felt like a lost opportunity. It was all too easy to get consumed by the routine of tour bus, concert hall and then tour bus again. After a gig, you could become accustomed to jumping into the coach with several packs of beer and smoking a few spliffs. People would often pass out in their seats, unable to find the motivation to crawl back to their bunks. It was far too easy to work a whole tour and not see anything of the areas that you were passing through.

That way of working fitted well for certain people. It didn't worry them, missing the places of interest that swept by. They would have their minds entirely focused on the stage and the performance coming rather than the sights. Mike had travelled most of Central Europe many times, but he still preferred to see as much of it as possible. Often that saw him staring through the windscreen of a tour bus in the middle of the night. It wasn't unusual to find him in a front seat, chatting to Liam Bruce, the driver, into the early hours of the morning. He would be content to watch the miles as they continued clicking away.

After all his years on the road, Mike Dean had become used to finding that the tour schedules didn't make much sense. He couldn't help questioning the booking policies of the agents. Did they have any understanding of motorways or driving in general? It often looked as if those tours had deliberately been set out to zigzag around Europe. It wasn't unusual for them to drive up and down the same stretch of motorway several times within a few days. One of the things that stood out on the Demon Eater's tour, was that the scheduling was well-ordered, although he had to admit that they were playing some strange venues at times. For once, there appeared to be a logical progression to the series of dates. As far as he could remember, they hadn't backtracked on themselves at all, if they had, he'd missed it.

One thing that did stand out, as far as Mike could see, was that they seemed to be running around the outskirts of Europe. They weren't going near the usually guaranteed markets of countries like Germany or Holland. As it was the first part of the tour, Mike guessed that those dates would come in the second half. He was aware that the next leg of the tour was still being worked on by the band's agent. None of them had seen any of that proposed schedule yet, they had no idea what areas it might cover. It wasn't unusual for them to only hear the full tour schedule a few days before they were due to set off. It would give little time to prepare, but Mike had become used to that and always had a bag half packed.

As the tour rolled on, Mike Dean kept a closer eye on Rick Fischer's movements than ever before. He noticed him disappearing on regular occasions during that time. It was impossible to follow him every time, so he tried to keep track of his movements. It was becoming such a frequent event that Mike kept notes about the times and places. He wanted to have a log of everything that he had experienced, something that he could look back on, if he needed to. He was still hoping that he would find some lead that might help him understand what was going on. In case more was to come out of the whole matter, he wanted to have a written log. As on the day that Mike had followed him in Gothenburg, he was usually away for between two and three hours at a time. He would always return without any explanation for his absence, acting as if he had never been away.

Mike was aware that some of those trips were most likely genuine tour business. There was always plenty of tour related admin for any tour manager to attend to. Among other things, there would be the regular banking of funds from the merchandising, which could build up rapidly. They couldn't risk having that amount of cash sitting around in the back of the coach. The general accounting that went with running a tour, could take a long time. At one point, Mike spotted Rick sliding out of the venue's stage door, the band were busy sound checking at the time. As they had the time to spare, Tac wanted to run through some of the new numbers that they had been working on. Mike decided to make his next move, although he was far too busy to follow Rick on that occasion. For no reason that he could understand, he had the urge to take the opportunity and slide away for a few moments. Heading for the coach, something told him that no one would be there at that time. It would give him time to continue his investigation into what was going on.

Mike Dean didn't have enough time to follow Rick on that occasion. If he'd had the chance, he would have taken it, determined to see what he was up to and if his behaviour had changed. On the spur of the moment, as he saw Rick disappearing out of the door, something had urged him to take a new approach. He wanted to try and find clues to what was going on, in his attempts to discover what Rick was up to. The situation was one that didn't sit right with him at all. The more he thought through it, the more mystified he was becoming. No matter how much he thought about it, he couldn't explain why it was preying on his mind in the way that it was.

The tour coach was locked when he arrived, telling him that it was empty as he had been expecting. Unlocking the rear door, he stepped inside. Not sure how long he might have before someone turned up, Mike Dean made his way towards Rick Fischer's bunk. Strangely it felt almost as if he was being led there, but at the first look he could see nothing of any interest. Each of the bunks had lockers beside them, a place where they could stash items that they wanted easy access to. For no reason that he could understand,

Mike found himself drawn towards Rick's locker. The doors were flimsy and insecure, although some people had secured theirs with padlocks. Using his own key and twisting it at an angle, Mike managed to open Rick's locker with little trouble.

A clutter of books, scraps of paper and general rubbish was revealed, the usual junk that collected in all the lockers. After a closer look, Mike Dean noticed a small black flight case standing at the side. Lifting it out, he placed it on the bunk and tried the catches, finding the lid to be fastened securely. As he took a step back from the bunk, he had no idea what to do next. At that moment, Mike noticed a faint smudge of white flowing over the catches and watched in fascination. It looked a little bit like a chalk thumbprint that was moving across the case. When he tried to open it for a second time, he found that the catches flicked up without a problem. Swinging up the lid of the case, he was able to reveal the contents.

Taking out a layer of stiff white foam, Mike Dean uncovered a collection of red bricks. They looked exactly the same as the one he had found buried in the ground of the Gothenburg graveyard. The bricks had been set out in a ridged plastic tray. There were around twenty empty spaces, where others had once sat. A fine red dust had accumulated in the corners of the tray to show where they had been. Mike could see that it looked as if it filled half of the case, so with great care, he lifted the layer out. Underneath he discovered a second tray at the bottom. The bricks sitting in the lower tray, which were a complete set, had a different design engraved on them. This new device looked like an intricate capital letter I, to Mike's eye.

* * *

It was a little after eleven o'clock on the morning of the

band's day off in Bucharest. Mike Dean was up early and spotted Rick Fischer darting out of the hotel lobby. He had been sitting on a bench in an alcove close to the foyer. Even from that distance, Mike could see that Rick looked flustered and on edge, as he rushed away. By that time Mike had all but given up on the idea of him making any move. The feeling that Rick was going to have a day off from his secret endeavours, had settled on him. He had become engrossed in reading the book that he had loaded on his phone, that he nearly missed him.

Grabbing his jacket from the bench beside him, Mike Dean jumped up and followed Rick out of the door. His job was far easier on that occasion as Rick was in a rush and didn't bother to look behind him. He darted passed the people he encountered, not glancing over his shoulder once. Making his way along the Boulevard Biruintel, Rick was oblivious to the idea that someone might be following him. On the previous trip, he had been vigilant, scanning the area behind him every few minutes. As had been the case in Gothenburg, it was obvious that he knew exactly where he was going. To make it easier for Mike, this time he was travelling on foot.

Strolling along a road that was carrying little traffic. Mike noticed a few scattered pedestrians as he followed in Rick's footsteps. Making slow progress, they wound their way up into the foothills of a forested area. The landscape around him contained deep shades of green on either side of the road. Glancing to his left, the view showed a steep downward slope. Over the treetops, he could see into the farmlands of the distant valley below. The scattered flocks of sheep and cattle and occasional buildings were all that broke up the view. Mike Dean had been following his quarry for what seemed like an hour or more. Looking away from the surrounding landscape, it was a surprise to find that Rick Fischer had disappeared from sight. Mike had been daydreaming about the possible outcome of their trek. Distracted by his thoughts, he hadn't spotted where Rick had turned off the road.

Becoming alert to the fact that Rick had dropped out of sight, Mike scrutinized the area before him. Could he have noticed him, while he had been walking along, not paying attention, he asked himself. Further along the road, he reached the spot where he had last seen Rick. Worried that his quarry might be lying in wait for him, somewhere nearby, he moved with a great deal of caution. A heightened sense of awareness took over, as he made a rapid inspection of the general area. On close examination, Mike spotted a thin trail heading off into the dense treeline. As far as he could tell, it was the only possible direction that Rick could have taken.

Mike Dean clambered over the railing that edged the road and set off along the muddy track that was in front of him. The whole area was suffering from the previous evening's torrential rain, there had been no time for it to dry out. Stumbling over roots and broken branches, he tried to keep to the thicker grassy areas at the side of the main trail. It was partly an attempt to stay as clean as possible but, he was also wary about leaving any tell-tale signs of his pursuit. If Rick Fischer was to return the same way, he didn't want to provide unnecessary footprints or any other marks. As he walked through the packed trees, he kept his eyes and ears on high alert for any signs that his target was near.

If Rick Fischer was ever to realise that he was being followed, Mike was in no doubt that he would have a hell of an explanation to come up with. The trail wound on through the trees and scrubby grassland but there didn't look to be any signs of life. At that moment he became aware of a clearing that had appeared, a few hundred yards ahead of him. Mike stepped further off the main trail and into the thicker undergrowth. The area was saturated after the evening's rain, soaking him as he forced his way through the dense foliage. He looked for a spot where he could see what was going on without being discovered.

Pushing aside some of the thicker branches, Mike Dean made a space that he could see through. As he peered into the gap, he was able to make out Rick Fisher in the distance. The man was down on one knee, an uncomfortable frown on his face, in the centre of the clearing in the trees. From his attitude, Mike couldn't help thinking that he was praying. That idea made Mike question, once again, what gods Rick could be calling on. What deities might inhabit a muddy woodland clearing in the depths of the Bucharest countryside, he wondered. The whole affair was beyond his comprehension. As he looked closer, Mike was able to make out the same dull white smudge that he'd seen in Gothenburg. It was hanging there as before, a few feet in front of Rick. He had turned his back to Mike, so he was able to push a little nearer in his attempt to see what was happening.

As he managed to squeeze through the undergrowth, Mike could hear Rick chanting to himself. It was little more than a faint murmur that reached his ears, one without any clarity. Rick had dug a small hole in the ground by that time, in the same way as he had done at the church in Gothenburg. Mike strained his ears to hear better but with little success. No matter how much he tried, he was unable to make any sense of the words and phrases being chanted. The odd words that did drift through to him were in some unknown language. Somehow, he couldn't help getting the feeling that there was an ancient spirit to them. As Rick's intonation continued, Mike noticed that the white smudge was pulsing with the rhythm of the chant.

Rick Fischer finished performing whatever private ritual it was that he was pursuing. He pulled himself back to his feet and gazed around the clearing. It looked as if he had become aware of the fact that someone was watching him. Rick's eyes flicked past the area where Mike crouched but it didn't look as if he had been detected. From the scowl that crossed his face, Mike had the suspicion that Rick was not happy about something. The whole time, he paid no attention to the white smudge hanging in front of him, giving off the impression that he couldn't see it. Mike froze where he was, crouching there in the damp undergrowth. He hardly dared to breathe, until at last Rick appeared to be sure that he was alone. A few moments later, he strolled out of the clearing and disappeared into the trees.

Staying exactly where he was, Mike Dean became rooted to the spot. For a time he was unable to move a muscle, as the tension of possible discovery flowed over him. After such a close call, he wanted to make sure that Rick had plenty of time to get away from the clearing. Only at that point would he be willing to investigate the area. Mike spent fifteen minutes crouched in the undergrowth, before he considered it safe to make a move. At last, with a deep breath, he decided that the coast was now clear. Pushing through the branches, he stepped out into the scrubby grass at the edge of the clearing.

As had happened in the Gothenburg churchyard, Mike Dean found a red brick buried in the ground. It had the Y shaped symbol carved into it, picked out in now solid black wax, like the one he had seen the first time. The same smell of rotting meat, which he remembered from before, hung in the air at the centre of the clearing. It made Mike gag with its pungency, once in the back of his throat, it stuck there and wouldn't go away. Pulling a note pad out of his pocket, Mike sketched out a copy of the brick that lay in front of him. He paid specific attention to its mysterious Y shaped symbol. He wanted to determine the significance of the figure, certain that it had to have some deep meaning.

There was no way that Rick Fischer could be going through all this on a whim, Mike Dean told himself. Surely he couldn't be doing it all for the hell of it; there had to be something more to it. With his task now completed, Mike covered the hole over again. Pushing the damp earth back down, he did his best to make sure that there were no obvious signs of him having been there. With the wet undergrowth it was hard to remove all the traces that he had been there. He left the clearing a few minutes later, heading back into the surrounding treeline. Mike was on edge all through the trip into town. He was half expecting Rick to leap out and confront him, demanding to know why he had been followed.

# Four

"The day after having claimed the old man's house as mine, I set to work.

"It was quite early the next morning, when I woke up, drowsy and a little disorientated. I'd had an uncomfortable night's sleep in the lounge, curled up on the sofa which was slightly too small for me.

"Well, I couldn't face any of the bedrooms that first night in the house.

"After a little bit of searching, I managed to find a stepladder stuck away at the end of the garden. I found it hidden behind the old rotten shed, covered in cobwebs and knotweed. Once I had it free and brushed down, I set about an all-out attack on the ceiling upstairs.

"It took me several hours but in the end I managed to uncover the hatch. It had been plastered over and carefully concealed. Must have been the old man's way of trying to hide it!

"Well, I found it!

"Yet another thing to draw me in, I thought. Was I reading too much into it all, I wasn't entirely sure at that time. Would he plaster it over purely to force me to search for it? Was he as clever as that?

"Course, once I'd found the hatch, everything from there on was relatively easy. I hacked away the plaster and shunted the cover up into the attic, revealing a dark hole in the ceiling.

"Next problem, the set of steps that I'd managed to find only gave me enough height to reach the ceiling. They weren't tall enough for me to be able to climb up through that damned hole.

"I tried grabbing the sides and hoisting myself up but it didn't work. I ended up knocking the steps over and falling on top of them. Covered in bruises and scrapes, I was off to the local tool shop for a proper ladder. There were some other bits that I reckoned I might need in any case.

"By that time, I was feeling a little less frustrated by the whole endeavour, I must admit. At least I could see that I was getting somewhere, if fucking slowly.

"Finally, a couple of hours later, I managed to get up there, up into the attic. I got up there armed with the super powerful torch that I'd bought from the tool shop.

"Fully equipped to explore, I discovered that the place was packed with boxes and bags of all sorts.

"Which one of them did I want? I had no bloody idea!

"I realised that I'd have to search through it all till I found something. I managed to unearth some pretty bizarre stuff up there though, half of it I scrapped straight away. Useless bunch of rubbish most of it was. Even uncovered a box of old school things of mine and a bag of Mum's old clothes, fuck knows why he kept them!

"I did find a large box of old photos though. That was interesting, other than the pics of me as a kid.

"There was one small folder in the box with pics of the old man. He was wearing a strange hooded gown and there was some of him with an odd horned headdress stuck on his bloody head!

"Had to laugh at how serious he was looking in those pics. He was standing there, glaring at the camera, like an extra from a bad seventies' horror film. Could that be what it was, I wondered, did he manage to play a part in some film? Couldn't remember him ever saying anything about things like that but I guessed that it was possible.

"I searched through that bloody attic for the rest of the morning and into the afternoon. At the point when I was becoming really pissed off with the whole thing, there it was in front of me.

"I'd shifted a pile of damp boxes of rubbish out of the way, when I found the dark blue suitcase underneath them. The moment I saw it, I just knew that it had to be the one that I was looking for.

"I dragged it over to the hatch and angled it down the ladder, nearly knocking myself out at the same time. It was bloody awkward trying to force it though the opening like that. Had to slide it through diagonally, while keeping balanced on the ladder. All the way down, I was waiting for it to topple over. At last, I managed to carry the case through into the lounge and then found that I had to cut it open. The catches were locked and there was no sign of a key, didn't even know where to look for one.

"What's the first thing I find when I managed to open it? That bloody gown, that's what! The one that the old man was wearing in them photos!

"Curiously, I took it out and held it up, couldn't help thinking that it felt odd to the touch. It was made of some roughly woven material, couldn't tell what, and it was kinda warm. Yeah, almost felt like it was alive, was going to squirm away from my hands. As for the hood, well, can't really describe that, it was kinda oily to the touch.

"There was a vaguely disgusting feel to the gown but there was also something, something, comforting about it, I suppose. Sounds crazy, don't it?

"Other things I found in that case?

"Well, there was a lot more pics of the old man in odd costumes; real fashion disaster he was. Then there was several greasy, half burnt, black candles rolling around in the bottom. God they stank something fucking awful! Ain't never smelt anything like it!

"There was the books too, or, I suppose booklets or leaflets might be a better description of them. Largely they was about magic in one way or another. The ones that caught my eyes straight away were about how to raise demons, yeah, demons!

"Ha! Can you believe it, the old man was a real nutter! Course, I always suspected it!

"Well, that was what I reckoned at the time anyway. Thing is, I kinda found myself being drawn in, getting hooked on it, something about it all just got into me. Was like some damned parasite burrowing under my skin.

"Once I'd worked through it all, I packed everything back into the case, wanting to keep it a bit tidy like. Last of all, I reached over for that damned gown again.

"Well, of course, I had to try it on, didn't I, before I stashed it away. Somehow, I couldn't resist it. That's when things kinda got a bit screwy.

"I swung the gown around my shoulders and straight away a kinda warm sensation came over me. The rough scratchy fabric felt instantly comfortable. It almost wrapped itself around me, like some long, lost lover.

"Got to admit it was enticing, I wanted it touching me.

"I walked out into the hallway, so I could look in the three-quarter length mirror that hung out there. What can I say, yeah, it kinda looked good on me. Course, I wouldn't be going down the pub in it, but it was okay. Bit gothic maybe, but okay. Could see why the old man like it.

"I pulled an old Alvin Stardust kinda pose in front of the mirror. Course I needed some leather gloves and a big ring but I thought it kinda suited me. That was when I felt for the hood.

"I flipped that damned thing up over my head and something hit me. Don't know what it was, but I was out instantly, out like a light.

"Next thing I know, it was coming up to eleven o'clock at night. I found myself laying on the hallway floor, in front of the mirror. Somehow, I'd managed to lose something like five hours!

"When I came too, I was feeling a little bit odd. I was slightly light-headed and a bit dazed. Bit like you get when you're recovering from a mega hangover and I've had a few of them, believe me. So, I should know, shouldn't I?

"I took that gown off and threw it over a nearby chair. It lay there, taunting me with its presence, summoning me to put it on again. Yeah, I actually couldn't shake the idea that it wanted me to put it back on! Had to forcefully pull my eyes away from the damned gown. At last, I managed to drag myself into the kitchen, I desperately wanted to make a cup of coffee, I needed something.

"My throat was raw and dry by that time and I drank several glasses of cold water, waiting for the kettle to boil. I sat there at the table with the cup clasped between my hands, losing all track of time. Somehow that coffee was stone-cold when I tried to take a mouthful. Don't understand where that time went, it just melted away.

"My mind had become lost in some crazy fantasy world. A world of magic, dark magic, alive with devils and demons and all sorts.

"Course, I didn't know what it all meant at the time. It was just strange visions, but they slowly swamped my head, taking over completely.

"It took a few days before I began to realise what might be possible. That was, if I was able to follow everything through. If I read all those papers that the old man had left stashed away in that case, the ones he told me to burn. Course there was no way I was going to do that. No way that I was destroying anything.

"Over the next few days, I barely left the house. I sat there and read through everything that the case contained. It's gotta be the most I've read in one lump, ever. I don't normally read nothing, always feels a bit pointless to me, when I can see things on the telly, on my phone. Why would I want to sit there and read?

"Still, those books of the old man's were different, totally different. They was a little bit difficult to read at times, I must admit, there was a lot of things I couldn't understand. I couldn't get my head around some of the ideas at first. They seemed really out there, but suddenly something just clicked.

"I never understood what changed but for some reason it all gelled together and made some kinda sense. I could see where it was all leading to and how I could achieve a kind of mastery of all this, this magic.

"That was also the first time that I sensed the presence that I told you about. It was faint back in those days, a kinda background feeling but it was there, I knew it was there.

"It was enough to cause me to regularly look behind me though. I wanted to make sure that no one was standing there, reading over my shoulder. Yeah, would you believe it, I was really getting twitchy! Didn't like that sensation at all, left me feeling a little uneasy about everything. I was finding myself jumpy and fitful, even though I told myself that I was being stupid, there weren't no one there.

"By that time, I was wearing the old man's gown regularly. Something about it had forced me into putting it on again and I felt, well… I gotta say it, I felt quite comfortable in it.

"Strangely, I found that those books made a bit more sense when I was wearing it, I could understand them all a little bit more. Course, I realise that's bollocks! Don't make no difference what I'm wearing when I read, does it? Thing is, it sorta felt comfortable, like it was the right thing to do.

"Some of what I read was quite obviously rubbish. There was a bit about some bloke called Anton LaVey and his Church of Satan, and of course there was that twat Aleister Crowley.

"Course I'd heard about him. That kinda stuff I binned straight away, waste of fucking time that, comic book stuff at best.

"The real material, the good stuff, well, that didn't have the names of who'd written them. A few of them looked as if they was written by hand, pretty hard to read, they was. Some of them had been typed and a few were even printed, but they was all old, very old.

"First thing they told me, I needed to build a pentagram to work from. Well, I decided that I would have to use the spare bedroom for that. I could lock the door then, when I'd finished doing things.

"The old man's room would have been bigger. It would have given me more space to work in, but I still couldn't face having to deal with that at the time.

"The spare room was virtually empty when I stepped inside, all it held was a bed in one corner, just a mattress on the base. I shunted that up on one end, and pushed it up against the far wall. There was a small cupboard too but it was full of rubbish. Dumped that in the garden, so it was out of the way.

"Needing a solid floor to work on, I ripped up the carpet, so I could get to the floorboards underneath. What do you think I found? I found an old, roughly outlined pentagram, yeah!

"I now understood why the old man had kept the room so empty. Still, it didn't look as if he had used it in many years. It needed a little bit of work to bring it up to scratch. By the end of the day, when I sat back in the local pub with a well-earned pint, I was happy with what I'd managed to accomplish. At last I felt that I was on the way, wasn't sure where I was going, but I was on the way.

"The next day things started to get more awkward. I was following the instructions in one of those booklets, collecting the bits that I would need. You see, it told me that I should have black, blood candles?

"Where the fuck was I going to get them, I wondered. Was pretty sure that my local Tesco's wouldn't have them on the shelf. After looking through them leaflets, I found a recipe to make my own, and I was on my way.

"Two days later I was ready at last, all set to perform my first ritual. It was going to be a ritual of initiation. It was something the books told me was the best place to start.

"The book said that this ritual would give me the power to go beyond the human body, to reach a higher state of being. It promised me a state that was beyond all limitations. Yeah, do you believe that?

"Suppose I could have bought some mushrooms or acid to do that, but I guess it wouldn't have been the same, would it?

"Well I did it, I stood there in the pentagram, lit them candles, and they stunk to high heaven. I carefully read out the words of the ritual. Must admit that I felt a bit self-conscious at first. Didn't really understand what I was saying, but, and I know this is going to sound fucking strange, I had a feeling that the gown knew. That it was helping me in some way!

"That night I slept really well, as well as you can stuck on a sofa. I still didn't like the idea of sleeping in any of the bedrooms, even my old one. I managed a good few hours' sleep, that was the most I'd had in days. It was about four o'clock in the morning when I woke up with the intense feeling that someone was in the room with me.

"I almost shouted out but somehow I managed to stop myself. I reached over and flicked the switch on the nearby table lamp.

"Nothing! There was no one there, obviously. Still, that feeling wouldn't go away, it was there hanging over me. There was the feeling that someone was watching me, and it stopped me from falling back to sleep.

"That's when I had this kinda daydream, I guess it was. It was about an old woman who was following me around. Everywhere I went, she followed me; I couldn't shake her off."

# Five

The Demon Eaters played a successful gig at the Control Club in Bucharest, a very popular venue. From there they moved on to Belgrade's Cultural Centre Grad, a small but great venue near the Sava River. All the shows had enthusiastic audiences turn up and the merchandise stall was getting busier by the day. After that show, the company took the ferry across the Adriatic and into Italy. Over the next three days they played some successful gigs. The crowds that turned up were modest but energetic and great to play to. The run of Italian dates came to an end with an amazing night in Rome at the Contestaccio Club. They played to a completely sold out crowd; it was by far the best gig of the tour up to that date.

Straight after the Rome gig, they headed off across the Tyrrhenian into Sardinia. This date was one that they all thought was a pointless addition to the tour. They were due to play what was proving to be a very slow selling gig. The venue was one that none of them had heard of in Sassari, to the north of the island. In direct contrast to the gig in Rome, that night turned out to be the worst one of the tour. It often seemed to go that way, an awful night following straight after a great night. It never seemed to work the other way around though. As had been predicted, few people turned up for the gig in Sassari. Only a couple of hundred punters turning up in a venue that could have held a thousand or more.

The one good point for the night, was that those who did turn up were enthusiastic. They did their best to create an atmosphere in the cavernous venue. To make things worse, the band had to battle against the acoustics of the hall, which were awful. With hardly anyone there, the room felt hollow and lifeless. They found it almost impossible to create any kind of atmosphere. Mike Dean could tell that Jacky, the band's sound engineer, was battling against the acoustics all night. After the show, the band spoke to some of the locals, who were hanging around backstage. They were reluctant to leave the venue too early and wanted to chat. The band soon found that the advertising for the show had only appeared in the city a few days before the gig.

By that time the constant ferry trips were taking their toll on all the crew and especially Tac. He had never liked having to travel by sea, at the best of times, preferring to fly even if it was only a short trip. As the tour manager, Rick Fischer had taken the brunt of Tac's disapproval. He was right in the firing line and Mike was sure that he must have felt as if he had a target painted on his back at times. Rick took another verbal battering from Tac, at the ferry port in the ancient city of Civitavecchia. He did his best to ease the situation, but there was little that he could do. All that he was able to tell Tac was that the band's agent had made all the bookings. The costings of trying to fly the band around would have made the tour impossible, he explained.

Rick Fischer went out of his way to remind Tac that, even with his reputation, this was a first tour for the band. At the end of the day, they were still a largely unknown band in most circles. They had to start somewhere and first tours could always be a bit up and down. The sound that they had was a completly different from anything that he had done before. It was all new and putting on a tour was not cheap. There was not much financial leeway floating about for things like flights. The extra outlay would have made the tour virtually impossible; they were barely making a profit as it was. With the previous bands that Tac had been in, he had been able to fly everywhere, but they had all been far bigger names. They had been playing to far larger audiences, and they could afford the extra expenses. In the scheme of things, The Demon Eaters were still an unknown quantity, even when you took into account Tac's name.

The experience of having to play to an empty hall on top of all the travelling by sea, had taken its toll. Tac was in a foul mood as the company set off the next morning. They now had to make the short trip towards the city of Porto Torres. From there they would have another ferry trip, this time across to Marseille. They managed to arrive reasonably early, and the crew sat around waiting for the ferry, as there was little else for them to do. Once Rick Fischer had booked them in, another argument sparked up between him and Tac. The war of words becoming more and more heated as it continued. The early afternoon sunshine took a hold, warming the air and the fragile tempers of the two men. Tac ranted on about the organisation of the tour, picking holes in everything that he could think of. He even threatened to leave the agency and find someone else who could look after his tour arrangements.

There was no way that any of them could help listening to the argument, as it escalated in front of them. Tac was becoming louder and more animated by the minute, as his frustration took hold. Although Rick Fischer was in the firing line, there was nothing he could do about the scheduling of the tour. Everything had been booked by the band's agent, months before. Rick was there to ensure that the day-to-day routine ran as smoothly as possible. As far as the previous night's non-event of a show was concerned, Rick tried to put up a logical argument. He tried to explain that there was little they could do if the local promoters didn't advertise the shows. At the end of the day, it was down to them, if they wanted to lose money on a booking. The band would still be paid their standard fee for playing the gig.

Rick Fischer reeled out the usual explanations, once more. Pointing out the tour costings again as he tried to explain things. In the end, mainly to keep Tac quiet, he said that he would talk to the band's management first thing the next morning, although he didn't know how much he could influence the situation. To counter Tac's increasing temper, Rick had one piece of information to give him, something that he'd been keeping to himself. The band's management had told him that they were working on a possible support tour with Nine Inch Nails. Somehow Trent Reznor had heard them and liked the sound that they were producing. It was early days, but he had enquired about their availability for a series of gigs that they were planning. The management had asked Rick not to mention it, as it was still some way from being confirmed. They were all aware that a tour supporting a band like that would help to get them where they wanted to be.

As the argument escalated, Mike Dean couldn't believe the strength of Tac's protests. He completely ignored the latest bit of news about Trent Reznor's interest in the band. The idea of supporting such a big name didn't seem to affect Tac's way of thinking, it was unlike him to go off like that. Having worked with him for so long, he found it hard to remember another time when Tac had become that upset. As it was about something that was, in the scheme of things, quite trivial, it seemed particularly odd. In the end Mike had to put it down to be a result of The Demon Eaters being Tac's own band. With that came the added pressure that he was now feeling from fronting his own line up. In the past, when he had been the lead guitarist in someone else's band, it hadn't meant as much to him.

* * *

They arrived at Espace Julien, the Marseille venue, after a fraught ferry crossing. By that time, even Mike Dean was feeling stressed and on edge himself. All that he wanted to do was carry on with the normal routine, and he set up his guitar corner, as soon as he could. He wanted to make himself busy as he tried to take his mind off the arguments that had now become frequent and stressful. The best way he knew was to lose himself in the job at hand, seeing to Tac's guitars. While the equipment was being set for the gig, Rick Fischer and Tac took off with the local promoter. They had a taxi booked to drive them to a nearby radio station. An interview had been arranged to help push the show, something that Tac was slowly becoming used to. It was another thing that was part of the regular routine, as the tour continued. More and more people wanted to hear about them and it was all good promotion for the band.

The pair returned to the venue a couple of hours later and it was obvious that something was wrong. The strained atmosphere between the two men was far more intense than it had been when they set off. Tac found the backstage area far too busy for his liking as he waited to sound check his gear. Storming off in a rage, he threw a cup of coffee across the passage, soaking a nearby security guard. Locked away inside the tour coach, Tac left Mike to complete the soundcheck for him. He refused to take to the stage to check his guitars or return to the venue. Rick Fischer walked onto the stage as Mike was setting Tac's effects pedals up. Unwilling to say anything, Rick refused to fill in any details about what had happened at the radio station.

As on any tour, when things started to go wrong, it didn't take long for stories to creep out over the grapevine. It was impossible to keep anything that had happened quiet for long. Mike Dean was able to make out some of what had taken place from listening to one of the local backstage crew. From the start of the interview, the radio presenter made a series of statements that Tac took offence to. Whether they were direct criticisms or the result of the presenter's awkward English, it was hard to tell. From what Mike heard, the argument centred around Tac's change in style. The fact that he had left his old glam rock persona behind him was something that the presenter didn't seem to like. He wanted to know the reason for the change and wasn't against telling Tac that it was wrong.

At first Tac tried to ignore, what he perceived as constant sniping, for as long as possible. He attempted to turn the interview back to the subject of The Demon Eaters and away from him past bands. After asking the presenter to change the subject for the third time, he let his frustration take over and lost his temper. Ripping off his headphones, he stormed out of the studio, knocking microphones out of the way as he went. The presenter followed Tac out into the corridor of the radio station, trying to calm him down. He didn't seem to understand what he had done to upset him, completely unaware that he had pushed it too far. In the end, with the presenter refusing to leave him alone, Tac had reacted. Turning around, he punched him in the mouth. It was something that bemused Mike, he had never known Tac to react like that in any situation.

The gig at the Espace Julien was well attended and the crowd responded to the band enthusiastically. Adding to the positive feeling, the merchandising stand was busy all night. They sold a great number of t-shirts, hoodies and baseball caps, depleting the stock levels. The whole night ended up being an extremely good one. It helped to push the memories of the disastrous Sardinian show into the background. Once the gig was over and the equipment stashed away in the backline truck, they were back on the road. They were now heading for their next gig in Bordeaux.

Reaching Bordeaux was something that both Mike Dean and Tac had been looking forward to. Sam and Wendy, their girlfriends, were travelling over for the gig and were going to meet them at the venue. Several years before, Mike had bought a camper van and the girls would often use it to follow the band around. It was something they tried to do, whenever they could find time away from their other commitments. They would be bringing a new consignment of t-shirts and other merchandise with them. After the Bordeaux gig, the girls were planning to stay on for the last few dates. The tour would move on through Nantes and on to the Élysée Montmartre in Paris before returning home. The Élysée was always a great venue to play and it would also mark the end of the first leg of the tour. From Paris they would have a welcome return to the UK and a well-earned break.

At the end of the Paris show, the band sat around in the backstage area, drinking. They were busy chatting to some of the locals that had invaded the dressing rooms, wanting to meet the band. As they were sitting there, Rick Fischer appeared with a sheath of paperwork in his hands. He wanted to run through the details for the return trip to the UK, he stated, ignoring the fans. As he explained the travel times and arrangements, Mike Dean could sense what was coming. He could see Tac rising to his feet, out of the corner of his eye. Straight away Mike recognised the signs that he was about to lose his temper. They were booked on the Cherbourg to Southampton ferry, later the next day, for the return trip to the UK. Hearing that, Tac said that he would not be making that crossing. Within moments he was shouting that it was out of order and rounding on Rick Fischer, once again.

As usual Rick tried to reason with him. He explained that the Paris date had been a late addition to the schedule, coming in at the last minute. Before that, Nantes would have been the final gig. Driving to Cherbourg would have been the logical way of doing things. Of course, Tac argued that as soon as the Paris date came through, the ferry bookings should have changed too. There had been plenty of time to make the alterations rather than leaving them as they were. The drive from Paris to Calais followed by the ferry to Dover would have been a far easier and quicker one. That was the one that they should be going for, Tac argued.

It was becoming clear to everyone that Tac was in no mood to back down. He was going to have his own way, one way or another. Even Sam found that she was unable to calm him down, something that she could usually do. After ten minutes arguing, Rick Fischer said that he would see what he could do. With a deep frown set on his face, he stormed off towards the venue's site office without another word. He was in a foul mood by that time, the constant battling with Tac was taking its toll on him. They all knew that Rick didn't like being on the losing end of an argument at the best of times. It became even worse when it was an argument with Tac.

The equipment was ready for their return to the UK, stacked away with tetris like precision. There was little else for them to do but sit around in the backstage area of the venue and wait. With nothing to do, several of them set about drinking from the well-stocked fridge of beers. They were waiting for a decision on what was going to happen next; everything was on hold. There was a strained atmosphere hanging over the crew, one that seemed impossible to break. The ongoing arguments and general tension that it had created had taken its toll on everyone. By then, they all needed some time out, before things really got out of hand. The chance to recharge their batteries and escape each other's company would revitalise them all, before they set out again.

Steve Rudge, the driver of the backline truck, was eager to set off as soon as he could; all he wanted to do was get home. It didn't worry him which crossing he was taking, as long as he could get on the road as soon as possible. He was anxious to set off, while the roads were still quiet, knowing that traffic could start building quite early. None of them could make a move until they knew where they were going. In the end they waited for around an hour, some of them drinking far too much from the copious supply of alcohol. In the end, Rick Fischer reappeared with an irritating smug expression, carrying a large notepad.

Glancing down at the pad, Rick Fischer flipping between three pages in silence. After a moment looking at his pad, he announced that he had been able to change some of the bookings. It hadn't been easy, he growled, glaring across the room at Tac. He would have to explain the alterations to the management once they got back, he snapped. There was no way that he was going to take the flak for the changes and the extra expenses incurred. With a brief glance at Tac, an expression of intense dislike on his face, he continued running over the details. Rick had managed to book the band onto the Calais to Dover ferry, as Tac had demanded. They would have a wait once they reached Calais, but they would have to put up with it, if that was the route they wanted to take.

Steve, with the Backline truck, would have to stay on the original Cherbourg crossing. Rick explained that he hadn't been able to change that booking, that would have been too complicated. At last everyone made their way out to the car park and their respective vehicles, keen to finally set off. As he reached the door, Rick stopped Mike and told him that he was going to travel with Steve on the Cherbourg crossing. He pushed the notepad with the band's rearranged booking details into Mike's hands. He would have to deal with the details, Rick said. It looked as if he had no intention of spending any more time with Tac than he had to. After the open hostility that had flared up between them, Mike wasn't at all surprised.

It was out of order for Rick Fischer to do that, to Mike Dean's mind, though he could understand it. At first, he refused to take on the role being forced on him but after considering it, he thought better. Rick was the tour manager and, as such, should stay with the band regardless of the arguments. Unfortunately, issues like that were part of the job, it was what he was being paid for. You couldn't drop things when you felt like it, but under the circumstance, Mike decided that it would be for the best. It was obvious that the latest disagreements with Tac were hitting Rick hard. Mike couldn't help wondering whether he would still be with the tour, when it restarted in a few weeks' time.

The band now had four weeks off, before the second leg of the tour was planned to start. Mike hoped that the time would give the situation a chance to calm down and return to a sense of normality. Having fourteen people living in each-others pockets was bound to create some tension. It was something that needed containing, otherwise everything could fall apart.

Mike had witnessed a few disturbing encounters during his time on the road. He was never too surprised when someone lost it, as people's egos and insecurities rose to the surface. Over the years, there had been times when he had been close to losing it himself. To his mind, those confrontations never did much to solve any of the underlying problems. If anything, they often resulted in a sacking or in someone walking away.

# Six

After driving through the night from Paris, they found that they had to wait for several hours in Calais. At last the band were relaxing on the ferry, heading towards Dover. Now that Rick Fischer had left with the backline truck, the whole atmosphere had changed. Mike Dean was sitting in the bar, enjoying a pint of lager and a large pack of salt and vinegar crisps. He watched the French coastline shrinking behind him, happy to be on the way home, at last. At that moment, Sam, Tac's long-term girlfriend came up and dropped into the seat beside him.

"What going on, Mike?" She asked in an undertone, not wanting anyone nearby to hear. "He hasn't been back on the gear, has he?"

Tac had a minor heroin problem at one point in his early days of touring. That had been several years earlier, at the time he had been playing guitar for a band who had all been using. It was something that he had been able to put well behind him, since leaving that band. It was one of the issues that had spurred him into moving on and start his own band. Mike Dean was pretty sure that he had no interest in anything like that any more. Having worked with him for so many years, he was certain that he would spot the signs. He tried to allay Sam's fears, but she said that there appeared to be something strange about him. He didn't seem to be himself, since she'd met up with them all in Bordeaux.

Now that the subject was out there, Mike had to admit that he had noticed a slight change in Tac. The main issue had been his attitude towards people in general. Mike had been conscious of the change but knew that the constant battles with Rick hadn't helped. Recently Tac had come over as a lot more argumentative than he had ever been before. He had even become violent as he had with the radio presenter in Marseille. He had never reacted like that to anything before, as far as Mike was aware. Sam hadn't heard about the incident in the radio station and it worried her even more when Mike told her about it. The whole thing was totally unlike Tac, she said, yes, he could be a little bit up and down at times, but couldn't everyone?

As the conversation continued, Wendy appeared with a glass of red wine in her hand. Seeing her approaching, Mike Dean switched the conversation onto other topics. Changing the subject, he told them about the secret trips that he had noticed Rick Fischer taking during the tour. Explaining how he had followed him and the strange way that he had been behaving. It was an issue that had been playing on his mind for weeks. By that time, he needed someone to talk to about it, someone to bounce his thoughts off. Without a sounding board, he was aware that his mind could blow the whole matter out of proportion. It was yet another strange twist in the normal tour routine, one that Mike had never come across before. Something that he couldn't force out of his mind, it was so abnormal.

Explaining about the case of engraved bricks that he had found in Rick Fischer's locker, Mike watched the expressions on their faces. At that point Sam became curious about the discovery. She asked several questions, wanting detailed descriptions of everything that he had seen. The question that had come to her mind, was why the bricks with the Y shaped design were the ones being used. Why not the bricks with the other figure, what was the difference between them, she asked. That was a question that had been on Mike's mind, for several weeks, but one that he had been unable to answer. The second layer of bricks, those engraved with what he described as being a stylised I, were intact when he had found them. Spotting Tac heading towards them, Sam suggested that Mike should talk to Richard Levi, when he got back to London.

Richard Levi was a good friend of Sam and Tac's. Mike Dean had met him several times over the years and always got on well with him. They would often meet him at one of the many parties that Tac held, when they were home. Richard owned a small bookshop in the Camden area. He specialised in anything that was a little bit out of the ordinary, the supernatural and occult making up a large part of his private collection. Before opening the bookshop, Richard had studied witchcraft, mysticism and the occult in general. After everything that Mike had told her, Sam was sure that it all fell into Richard's field of expertise. It was the type of thing that he loved investigating, and he always had stories to tell about the things that he had found.

Everything that Mike Dean had seen and heard definitely fitted Richard's field of expertise. It all sounded as weird as some of the stories that he had told them about over the years. Whenever he turned up at parties or a night in the pub, he would always have a great range of tales to tell. Those stories were almost always based around incidents that he had encountered himself. Mike had to admit that it sounded like a good place to start. He didn't know where else he could turn and at least speaking to Richard couldn't do any harm. Who knows, he might be able to shed some light on the whole episode, Mike thought. If nothing else, it would give him something to concentrate on over the four-week break. It would be something to occupy his mind before the tour kicked back into action.

* * *

Mike Dean began his first day back at home in London by going through a large pile of unwanted junk mail. Wendy had put it all to one side for him, in case there was something important hidden among the waste paper. She was unwilling to dump it all in the bin on the off chance that there was a vital document among the general rubbish. His second job of the day was the ordeal of sitting in the local launderette for what felt like hours. The large collection of extra t-shirts that he came home with after every tour always puzzled him. He set about loading the machines with the pile of clothes, wondering, as always, where they had all come from. Their washing machine at home was fine for smaller loads but it struggled with anything much bigger. Although it was all part of the usual post tour routine, it still dragged on. That was one job that he knew he couldn't put Wendy through. The whole operation was a minor nightmare but it did give him time to catch up on his reading while he sat there.

During all that time, images of Rick Fischer digging holes in the ground kept flooding back into his mind. No matter how hard he tried to ignore them and focus on reading his book, they wouldn't leave him alone. What had he been up to, Mike asked himself and was it anything that was worth making an issue about? He was unable to relax that first night back at home, he felt on edge and didn't sleep at all well. Questions concerning the things that he had seen kept rolling around in his head. In the end, shortly after three o'clock, he walked through to the lounge and put the television on. He had given up on sleep but didn't want to disturb Wendy with his restlessness.

When Wendy asked about his plans, the following morning,

Mike said that he had decided it was time to follow Sam's advice. He would pay Richard Levi a visit and see if he could come up with an explanation for what had been going on. Wendy agreed that it felt like a good place to start, if he wanted to uncover the possible motives behind Rick Fischer's strange behaviour. With that said, she rushed off to work, leaving him to think about it some more. It didn't take long for the whole issue to solidify in his mind. The moment that he settled on the idea, he found that his previous tension began to ease.

Meeting up with Richard Levi had always been a pleasure and was something that Mike Dean looked forward to. Richard was a large awkward figure, who seemed to constantly be on the verge of colliding with things. Being a sociable, happy-go-luck character, he was able to laugh off his innate clumsiness. It was a problem that he had grown up with, but he was well aware how it must look to other people. Richard's dress sense, or lack of it, always amused Mike. He frequently looked as if he had dressed in thirty seconds flat with the lights off. Colour co-ordination and ironing were things that bypassed Richard's cluttered mind. He had no interest in anything like that.

Mike received a warm welcome from Richard, when he stepped through the door of Levi's Books. It was his first visit to the shop; he had never been able to find the time before. Having phoned through that morning, to make sure that Richard would be around, they had been able to agree on a time. Within moments of his arrival, Richard led Mike through to his office at the rear of the shop. The rather dingy and cluttered room that he entered, was what served as the centre of his operations. Mike was led through the chaotic maze of shelving, wondering at the collection of books. Wherever he looked there were piles of them, stacked in every conceivable corner of the room. He even found that he had to divest a chair of its contents so that he was able to sit down.

"It's good to see you, Mike" Richard Levi said. As he spoke, he showed him the label on the bottle of Irish whiskey. He had removed it from a cabinet as he passed by, before pouring two large glasses. "So, what drags you all the way over here, and on your day off too?" He asked, as Mike hadn't gone into any details on the phone.

"Well, you know I've been out with Tac on The Demon Eater's tour." Mike started, wondering whether he was about to make a fool of himself. He was still not sure that what he was going to tell Richard was worth raising. Taking a sip of his whiskey, he continued. "Well, something doesn't sit right about the way that Rick Fischer's been acting. Don't know if you remember meeting Rick, at Tac's party the other month. He's the new tour manager?"

"Oh yeah! I remember him well. Couldn't forget him, could I?" Richard said. The intonation of his words said far more than the words themselves. "Didn't like the dude. From the first moment I met him, I felt there was something uncomfortable about him. Have to be honest, something about him gives me the shivers. I can't put my finger on it but, well… something about him spooked me. So, what's he been up to, Mike?"

"Well, it started when I noticed that he was sloping away on occasions, it was all rather secretive. It seemed to be happening almost every chance that he got." Mike said, as he began to relate his story. "Then I decided that I would follow him, if I got the chance."

"Okay, so, what was he up to?"

"Well, when that chance came, we were up in Gothenburg. I watched him bury an odd-looking brick in the grounds of an old church on the outskirts of the city. He went on to light a strange candle over it, then after a few minutes he stamped it all down and ran off."

"That's rather curious, I can see why it's caught your attention." Richard Levi said. He took a large mouthful of his own whiskey, spilling droplets down his shirt front. "Did you managed to find anything else?"

"Yeah, for some reason I found myself drawn to his locker on the tour coach. When I managed to get into it, I found a flight case with a pile of those bricks. There was also a layer of bricks with a completely different design on them."

"Yeah, must admit that sounds odd, Mike."

"The strange thing is, when I first tried to open the case, the catches wouldn't budge. I'm sure of it, I tried the catches several times, they wouldn't move. Then I tried it again, a few moments later, and the catches flicked open." For some reason Mike didn't want to mention the odd white light that he had seen flowing over the case. He was still not sure that he hadn't imagined the whole incident.

Mike finished his confused account of everything that he'd seen and looked over at Richard to see his reaction. Picking up a notepad and a rather ornate looking fountain pen, Richard drew something on the page with a couple of elaborate flicks of the nib.

"Those designs… the ones that you saw on those bricks." He said. "Were they anything like these?" He asked, turning the notepad round on the table and pushing it towards Mike.

Taking the pad in his now shaking hands, Mike looked down

at the two sketched drawings. "Yeah, you've pretty much got it, that's exactly what I saw!" He exclaimed. "How the hell do you know them? Do you know what they mean?"

Richard Levi leapt to his feet and darted out of the office door, colliding with the door frame as he passed. Instructing Mike Dean to stay put, he said that he would be back in a moment. Mike could hear a distant commotion out in the shop, followed by Richard telling his assistant that he would be busy for a while and that he didn't want any interruptions. When he returned to the back office, Richard was carrying a large atlas. He placed it on the table, after pushing a few notepads and books onto the floor, where they joined an untidy pile. Opening the atlas, he flicked through to the pages that showed most of Europe.

"Right, let's start this at the beginning." He said, with a gleam in his eye, showing that he was in his element. "Where did the tour kick off?"

As Mike Dean flicked up the diary on his phone, he ran through the tour schedule, date by date. With every place mentioned, Richard Levi marked a cross in the atlas, showing each city that the tour had visited. It wasn't long before they could both see a natural progression to the collection of crosses. They were describing an almost perfect circle on the map.

"Well, I guess that goes some way to explaining why we've been playing some strange venues on the tour." Mike Dean said, looking at the pages in front of him.

"Rather curious, isn't it, Mike?"

"Yeah, I thought it was some kind of first tour syndrome, getting to play almost anywhere that would have us." Mike Dean said, staring down at the map. "There must be a reason why the tour's been set out like this, it can't have happened by chance."

"Oh, I completely agree, Mike. This is no random chance event; this has taken some careful planning." Richard stated, tapping the map with his finger.

As he studied the map laying on the table in front of him, Richard Levi became lost in thought. He traced the circle on the atlas with his finger, lost in his own thoughts. Jumping to his feet suddenly, he strode across the room to one of the larger bookcases. Unlocking the ornately decorated glass doors, he picked out various volumes. One by one, he flicked through the books, then he would either return it with a tut and a shake of his head or put it on the growing pile beside him.

It was clear that Richard was searching for something specific, as he mumbled away to himself. Once again, he became completely lost in thought as he worked. Mike Dean sat there watching his progress, wondering what he was looking for. He sat in silence, waiting for Richard to say something. In the end, after around ten minutes spent watching his search, Mike spoke up.

"Richard, have you got some idea about what's going on here?" He asked, becoming a little annoyed by Richard's silence.

"Sorry? Oh, sorry, Mike. I well… I can't be sure about any of this at the moment, Mike." Richard said, spinning round on his heel. Mike couldn't help feeling that he had forgotten that he was there. He nearly dropped the pile of volumes that he had collected and that were roughly balanced in his arms. "But those designs that you described, well, they remind me of the Hebrew letters, noun and aein."

"Yeah, okay, if you say so." Mike replied, unsure of what that meant and what it had to do with anything.

"Now, there are some questions that come to my mind. First, why would Rick Fischer have bricks with Hebrew letters engraved on them? The other big question is, what is he doing with them and why?" Richard asked, pointing the corner of one of the books that he held in his hands towards Mike.

"Sounds as if you might have an idea…"

"Well, we need to twist things about a bit. Let's start looking at them from a Cabbalistic point of view. The letter noun can also stand for the fourteenth card of the Tarot; Temperance. Going with that flow, aein, the other letter stands for the sixteenth card; The Tower."

"Okay… does, does that get us anywhere, Rich." Mike Dean asked. Glancing down at his watch, he noticed that the afternoon was disappearing fast.

"Well, I'm trying to pull this all together in my head, and I'm, I'm not quite sure where it's going at the moment." Richard admitted, tapping on a page in the book he was holding. "Looking at the meanings behind those two tarot cards. In some ways they stand for completely opposing ideas. Where Temperance stands for regeneration and renewal, The Tower shows crisis and upheaval."

"Yeah, okay…" Mike Dean said, lost in what Richard Levi was trying to tell him. "So, where does that get us, Rich?"

Richard Levi continued for some time, often talking more to himself than to Mike. He opened and closed several books, glanced at them and put them aside. By the time that Richard had come to the end of his searching, the whole office appeared to be swamped with open books. His desk was full of scraps of paper, with scrawled notes on them, adding to the general chaos. Returning the books back to their rightful places, one by one, Richard asked about the second leg of the tour. Wanting to know where that would be taking them. As Mike hadn't seen the itinerary yet, he was unable to give him that information. All he could say was that he would tell him, once the dates became available.

"This whole thing seems to be operating on a different level." Mike Dean said, thinking about everything that Richard Levi had hinted at. "The whole scale of this seems to be far more than a rock tour. You seem to have posed more questions than you've actually answered, Rich."

"Yeah, I'm sorry about that." Richard said, with a faint grin that told Mike Dean that he was loving every minute of it, adding. "You know, I've been thinking about Rick Fischer. He might be doing his thing with those bricks and candles but he couldn't have booked the actual tour dates, could he? At the end of the day, he's only a tour manager."

"Yeah, the tour was the work of Toni Sillwood; she's the band's main agent."

"Toni Sillwood? I've met her, Mike, I'm sure I have. At one of Tac's parties. The name definitely rings a bell but I can't actually place her at the moment."

"So, you think Toni's involved in this too, Rich?"

"Well, to my mind, someone at the agency has to be behind this, somehow, if not Toni herself." Richard Levi said. "There would be no other way of getting these things linked up like this otherwise."

Mike Dean left Levi's Books, at around eight o'clock that

evening. Before leaving, he agreed to inform Richard about the new dates for the second leg of the tour, as soon as he could lay his hands on them. They both wanted to see how those bookings would fit in with the ones they had mapped out in the atlas. How would they fit into the circle, would they show something new?

# Seven

"Well, I finally managed to infiltrate that group, the one that I'd been trying to get into for ages.

"It all took a little bit of time, had to be careful. Couldn't let them know what I was really trying to do, could I? But I got in there in the end, knew I would.

"The Union of the Mountain Ash, as they call themselves, bloody stupid name that is. Had to be a bit devious to work my way in there. It all came together when I found an old mate of mine who had a mate who was linked to them and I had a great way to get at him. See, he loved his gear, he did, and I could supply it.

"Well, I twisted arms, wormed my way in, always been good at things like that. I sold him some dodgy gear, course that meant I had something to hold over him, well, then he kinda had to do what I asked, didn't he?

"Then again, I was saying about names. That lot in Germany, the Star of Destiny, they ain't much better, are they?

"Star of bloody Destiny, where'd they get that name from, fucking stupid name that is.

"At least I can understand them a little bit, I can kinda grasp where they're coming from. Let's face it, there's enough people in the country already, ain't there? Why'd we need them foreign infiltrators taking all the jobs; it's as bad there as it is over here.

"Them at the Union are beyond me though, they talk the same crap all the time. We're gonna save the world? We're gonna help humanity? We're gonna make everyone equal? We're gonna overthrow evil? Fuck off!

"Anyway, I'd been in there for a few months, acting all quiet like. I was watching what was going on and gaining their trust, making myself useful, then they said they had a job for me, if I wanted it. They kinda had the idea that it might be right up my street.

"By that time, they knew a bit about my past, what I let them find out anyway. They knew that I'd worked in the music business for a while, been a bit of a tour manager for a couple of dodgy bands. What I didn't tell them was, I did it as a way of selling gear. That way I could sell both to the bands and the punters, made a few quid out of that, I did.

"Well, the Union's plan was to use some rock group's tour as cover for what they was trying to do.

"Rock band? God awful noise is what I call it, fuck knows why anyone would want to pay money to listen to that garbage! Still, I've worked with worse, I think.

"And the people, god, where do they come from? They're a right bunch of losers, they are, especially that Tac bloke, but I think I can make use him. He's weak, he is and that could be useful.

"Gotta be a little bit careful with that Mike geezer, though, he's pretty close to Tac and could prove to be a problem. Yeah, I'll have to be wary of him, shouldn't be a issue as long as I'm careful.

"Lucy, the drummer of the band, well, she ain't no fucking problem. All she cares about is hitting things and staring at her damned iPad. She's fit though, I'll give her that. And Dave, the bass player, he's got headphones on and his head in a book most of the time that he ain't up on the stage.

"Rest of the crew, well, they're all the normal music types. Too busy with setting up gear and breaking it all down again, sound checking and tuning the stuff. Gotta feel sorry for them, having to listen to that crap every fucking day. There's gotta be a better way of making a living, still, each to their own, I suppose.

"They're always occupied with loading gear into the venues, then packing it all back into the vans. Far too many things going on for them to notice me. They ain't got the time to pay any attention to what I'm up to, and that's fine by me. Hopefully that means that I can pretty much ignore them too.

"Anyway, the people at the Union told me that they wanted these, things distributed around Europe. They called them talismans of power, said it was a way to create a protective aura, to help stabilise the area.

"Well, that was it, once I heard that, I was on it. Yeah, gave me a great idea that did.

"It was a way for me to get on with my plans. I could do what I wanted to do, and believe me, that's nothing to do with protection. The talismans that they handed me was a bunch of bricks with power symbols carved on them. That's what that Toni woman from the union explained, when she ran through what they wanted me to do with them.

"Well, that was exactly what I was looking for. That gave me the link to how I could get my thing going; I'd been a bit stuck for ideas up till then. Wasn't sure how to move on.

"You see, I knew that I had to generate my own source of power, needed it if my plan was going to work. In the end, I managed to get a bunch of bricks of my own made. They was like the ones they gave me but had to carve these up myself.

"I realised I was taking a risk using the same place to get them made, but it just had to be done. I couldn't see a way around that. Having them do the carving though, that would have flagged up as being odd, sure I couldn't have got away with that, so had to do it myself.

"My own power symbols, ones that would work for me, do what I wanted. Course, it took a good few days to do it; they had to be done properly, you see. Was while I was working on those bricks that I started to sense that presence again. That's when I became certain that it was a woman, although I don't really know how I could tell that.

"One evening, just as I was finishing off the last of them bricks, I saw something. First it was just that odd feeling again, the feeling that I wasn't alone, that I was being watched. I instinctively glanced over my shoulder a couple of times. Fuck knows what I was looking for, I knew I was on my own.

"Usually when that happens there's nothing there. That night though, I caught something out of the corner of my eye. It was a brief blur of white in the corner of the room, bit like a thumb print on a window. I attempted to focus on it but it was impossible, the more I tried to focus, the more it didn't seem to be there.

"Look, I'm losing track again ain't I?

"I was going to tell you about the band, The Demon Eaters. Well, at least that's a bit of a fun name for a band, ain't it? No one's going to be eating my demons though, I'll tell you that for nothing.

"Well, it's that Tac geezer I'm working on, he's the band leader. I've tried to be friendly with him, tried to get on, tried be the nice tour manager. It's not easy all the time though, he can be a right twat when he wants to be. Thinks he's god's gift to rock'n'roll, he does, obviously ain't heard of Keith Richards, has he. Keith would blow him back to wherever he came from, real musician he is, real rock'n'roller.

"As I was saying, I started sticking a little something into Tac's drinks during the tour. It was just a bit of a softener here and there, something that would make it easier for me to control him. I know I've got the power to dominate most people but it can take a lot out of me, leave me feeling drained. A little sweetener don't go amiss sometimes, makes it a little easier for me to do my thing.

"Course, I realised I could make use of him once I found out about his daughter. Oh yeah, that was a real eureka moment that was. Cheyenne, Tac's daughter! Finding out about her was spot on, she will be the perfect final piece to the jigsaw, round things out nicely, she will.

"I almost lost it at the end of the last set of dates, I must admit. What with Tac shouting at me like that, in my face all the fucking time. Telling me that he weren't going to take that Cherbourg crossing, as had been booked.

"It was all scheduled that way for a reason, of course. I had to plant them talismans in the right places, going to Dover would throw the whole fucking thing out of sync. Course, I couldn't tell him that now, could I? In the end, just as a way of getting some peace and quiet and to get him off my back, I changed the band's travel arrangements.

"At least that got them out of my hair for a bit. I could feel myself starting to lose control by that time. I told myself that if I lost it, I would ruin everything that I'd been working towards, I had to calm down. Had to get myself under control.

"I couldn't afford to do anything to mess up my progress, not when I was close to finishing the first stage of my plans. Once I got back home, I'd have a couple of weeks away from them bastards, get my head together. That would give me time to focus on the next part of my plan, cos that was important that was, very important.

"There was a lot that needed to be done to get these rituals right. You can't just wing it and hope it'll work out the way you want it to.

"That said though, I'm finding that I can improvise with them a little bit. A little bit here and there, especially on some of the more basic rituals. Guess what, they're working out fine. So, maybe I'm becoming good at this, after all, growing into it, mastering the whole thing.

"Yeah, I'm gonna rule the world, I am! Gonna take control of everything!

"Well, at least that's something I can thank the old man for. Without him, I'd never be where I am now, would I? Still, I'd love to know if he deliberately set me up with this, as I suspect he did. Led me by the nose, certain that I wouldn't be able to resist it, that I'd do just what he wanted me to do.

"If he did do that, well, all power to him, he was a damned site cleverer than I ever gave him credit for. Maybe I could find a ritual to bring him back, then I could ask him it. Thinking about it though, na, don't think I really want to see him that much.

"Oh well, only got to keep my nerve for a little bit longer, then I'll be off and running. I'll really be able to cause some havoc then, won't I? Got to see it through to the end of this bloody tour now, no choice. I'll never have to see any of them again, once it's over, other than Tac but that'll only be for a short while, obviously.

"By the time we get to that stage, he'll be so under my control that I won't need to worry about him at all. I'll use him for what I want, then he can fuck off with the rest of them. I won't ever have to see him again.

"Some of these rituals need some really strange stuff. Things like blood, that's always a favourite that is, and not any old blood; has to be a little bit special. Bit of a challenge that one is, but I can handle it, there's always a way. You just have to know how.

"When I'm standing there beside Baphomet. I'll be his right-hand man, well, then people will really take notice of me, won't they? They'll all know who I am then and they'll pay for the way they've treated me in the past.

"They all took the piss out of me at school, 'Look, here he comes, Rick the Dick.'. Yeah, I remember them all, how they treated me. Well, they'll soon be paying for that, won't they?

"I'll rub their bloody noses in it, treating me like that and them at the factory, they was no better, was they? Just cos I didn't want to join them at the pub after work, or go into that damned canteen for lunch. I had nothing in common with them losers, no reason for me to hang out with idiots like them.

"Course when I told the foreman to stuff his job, that just made them worse. Especially as we all lived in the same kinda area. I'd run into them regularly, in the local shops, in the streets, in the pubs. They'd be there pointing at me behind my back, talking about me when I couldn't hear them, laughing at me. Course they'd never let me see any of that, would they?

"If I turned around to confront them, ask them what they had against me, well, they'd act all normal like. As if they weren't taking the piss out of the way I walk, the way I dress, the way I talk, but I knew, yeah, I knew.

"Well, they know nothing! Soon they'll know though, yeah, soon they'll bloody know. When I raise him, when I bring him into this world, then they'll all pay for the way they've treated me."

# Eight

The previous day's meeting with Richard Levi hung like a dull weight on Mike Dean's mind. The more he ran through everything that he had listened to, the more uncomfortable he became. He couldn't get what he had heard out of his head, it all rolled around in there, keeping him awake most of the night. It had been quite unsettling to see the tour dates set out on a map in front of him like that. The near perfect circle surrounding the main body of Europe seemed somehow threatening, it felt ominous. He was sure that there had to be a reason behind it but had no idea what it could be. Surely something like that couldn't happen by chance but what that reason could be, was beyond him. He had no idea how or why something like that might come about or why anyone would want to make it happen. By midday, he had become so restless that he wasn't comfortable anywhere. He was slowly becoming ever more annoyed by sitting around, letting it all run through his mind.

In the end, Mike Dean decided that he was going to do something positive. Trying to settle on something that might help the situation, he came to the decision that he would phone the band's agency. He was hoping that he would be able to speak to Toni Sillwood and find out the next set of dates from her. His first call got no further than an unhelpful, disinterested, switchboard operator. On his second attempt, he found himself put on hold for what felt like hours. The bland electro-pop playing in the background, made the wait seem far longer than it was. At the moment when he was about to hang up, he was put through to Toni Sillwood. Mike had never got on with the woman, although he'd only met her once or twice. He was aware that they had little in common, so made his request for the tour dates without much preamble.

Mike knew that his vague dislike for the woman might partly be due to her being an agent. There was something about agents in general that always grated on him. He could never shake the feeling that they would push a band to their limit, regardless of the consequences. There appeared to be little understanding of what they were doing to them in the process. All they saw was the money to be made from a tour and little else. The personal effect on the band members and crew always seemed to come second to them. It seemed to be the case that a booking was a booking, in an agent's mind. They would take the gig even if it meant that the band had to double back over hundreds of miles. Often it meant that they ended up playing in venues that were not unsuitable or the wrong size.

Toni Sillwood proved to be pleasant enough on the phone, when Mike finally spoke to her. Her broad London accent came over the phone with an enticing edge to it. She tried to make some initial small talk, asking about the tour and the audience reactions. After several minutes of meaningless conversation, Mike asked her about the new dates. Toni told him that the gigs for the second part of the tour were pretty much finalised. Although there could be a couple of late additions to the list, if everything went as well as expected. If Mike wanted to see it straight away, Toni said that she could have them emailed through to him. He would have them within fifteen minutes or so, she told him. Making sure that Toni had the correct email address, Mike thanked her and said his goodbyes. As he shut his phone down, he began to think that he might have misjudged her.

The next half an hour Mike spent in front of his laptop, waiting for the promised email to arrive. The time dragged on endlessly, making him think that it had stopped altogether. It was only when he left the room that he heard the tell-tale ping of his inbox. By that time, he was about to step into the shower, having decided to go out for a walk, anything to pass the time. On a quick glance through the list, Mike's first impression was that it took in a lot more of the usual European venues that he was used to. The type of towns, cities and venues that he would have expected them to be heading for. There were also return visits to some of the places that they had already played. He had to admit that was a little strange. Playing too often in the same area was usually bad news, considering they had played a couple of them less than two or three months before.

The regular areas of Holland, Belgium and Germany were all in there, including many old favourites. Mike recognised most of the venues, places that he had worked in before. A few of the gigs were new to him, but that would always happen. Venues often closed down or changed their names on a regular basis. As he ploughed through the list of information, Mike Dean couldn't see any problems with the schedule. If anything, it was far more like the usual tour schedule that he would have expected. The whole thing seemed to be set out in giant zigzags that ran across the European landscape, as far as he could see.

After an afternoon of shopping, Mike Dean made his way through the dense crowds of Camden Town. Negotiating vast mobs of sightseers and shoppers, he worked his way towards Levi's Books once again. He had phoned Richard Levi several hours before to tell him about the new dates. After the call, he had sent a copy of the email that he'd received from Toni Sillwood, with all the dates. Mike couldn't wait to find out whether Richard had been able to spot anything in the list that he hadn't noticed. Richard's assistant, Jamie, was at the counter when Mike walked into the shop. He was busy serving a woman with a large pile of paperback books and looked rather distracted. As Mike approached the counter, Jamie sent him straight through towards the office. Richard was waiting for him, he said, before returning to his customer.

Once again, the atlas was laying open on the Richard's cluttered desk. It was one of the first things that Mike Dean saw as he walked into the packed and chaotic room. Richard was there, hunched over the open book, with a marker pen clenched in his hand. The moment he looked at the atlas, Mike could see the circle from the previous night had now been highlighted in bright red pen. It now stood out far more, glowing in its ferocity. A printed copy of the email that Mike had sent through was laying on top of the map. Richard was busy crossing off the dates. He was marking them out with an orange pen to differentiate them from the red of the circle. Glancing over his shoulder, Mike saw that he was adding a series of arrows after each of the crosses. The arrows were there to show the direction that the tour was taking.

Looking up from the atlas before him for a second, Richard Levi waved Mike over to the table without a word. For the next few minutes, he continued plotting out the tour dates until all the gigs on the list had an orange cross. Finishing his task, Richard took a step back from the table and stretched. Tapping the end of his pen on his forehead, he appeared to be lost in thought for a few moments. He stared at the map with its scattering of orange crosses but said nothing at that point. There was something in the expression on his face that Mike hadn't seen before, it seemed to be a mix of exhilaration and extreme discomfort.

"All looks pretty normal, don't it?" Mike said. The question was asked more to break the silence than anything. He couldn't help feeling that the expression he could see on Richard's face was saying that he found it far from normal.

"Oh, I don't know if you can call this normal, Mike. Not normal at all." Richard replied in an undertone. Having finished his marking, he put the pen down on the table and watched as it rolled onto the floor.

"I don't understand, Rich... can you see something that I can't?"

"Oh, there's a definite pattern beginning to emerge here." Richard said, picking up the pen from the floor and grabbing a ruler that was sitting on a pile of books, he added. "Take a look at this, Mike."

Placing the ruler on the map, Richard Levi drew an orange line that joined several of the crosses. The line continued from Nottingham through to Vilnius in Lithuania, with one sweep of the marker pen. They could see that several of the crosses came quite close to the line. The cities marked out included Gdansk and Hamburg. After the first, Richard drew a second line, running from Vilnius to Toulouse. Once again, it linked several more of the crosses, like some giant kid's dot-to-dot book. Adding another three lines to the map, Richard lifted it up to show Mike what he had done. They could both see that most of the crosses were now linked up.

Mike Dean couldn't help thinking that it looked like something out of a child's colouring book. Tac's daughter, Cheyenne, had a collection of them, and she loved colouring the pictures that she completed. The image that appeared in bright orange was that of a giant five-pointed star. The vivid lines making it stand out against the green and white of the European land mass.

"Well… there you go, Mike." Richard Levi said taking a deep breath and sitting down heavily in a nearby chair. The chair creaked against the sudden weight and for a moment threatened to topple over. "I think we may have found a bit of a clue here. Something's definitely going on and, I suppose, we should investigate it a bit further. I don't think we can leave this one alone"

"But what reason could there be for setting the tour out in this way?" Mike asked, feeling bemused by the latest development. He didn't quite believe what he saw laid out in front of him. "I don't see what this all means. And anyway, couldn't you link those spots up to create almost any shape?"

"Oh no, Mike. It doesn't work like that at all. You might not have noticed it, but I joined them up in the order that they've been set out in. This has all been very carefully thought out."

"So, what do you think it means, Rich? Have you got any ideas about that?"

"Well, the pentagram, like the symbols that you found carved on those bricks, can have opposite meanings." Richard began, tapping the centre of the atlas with his finger. "You could use it as a form of protection, but it can also be destructive and used to shock. It all depends on the people using it and what they're trying to achieve."

"You've lost me, Rich." Mike said, shaking his head in bemusement. "I don't understand any of this. It seems like something out of some old Hammer film, have you got Peter Cushing hiding out back somewhere?"

"Mike, I'm thinking about those bricks that you saw and the way that Rick was using them. Well, the ones with the symbol for aein on them, well… that doesn't seem like a very good sign to me."

"Why not, Rich? What are you getting at?"

"Well, whoever's setting this up seems to be intent on creating some kind of upheaval, that's if I'm reading the signs right."

"But what makes you think that, I don't see it?"

"The pentagram that we've marked out here takes in most of central Europe. I can only think that they're trying to create an unstable aura over the area for some reason. Although I must admit that I've got no idea why or who for that matter."

After some discussion they tried to decide on what they should do next. Richard suggested that the first step should be for Mike Dean to taking a trip to the agency in Hammersmith. With luck, he would be able to speak to Toni Sillwood in person. He could see if there was anything that he could find out from talking to her face to face. It was late that evening when Mike made it home, after a distracted trip on the tube, where he took off in the wrong direction at first. Having to jump off at the next station and double back on himself, was a stupid mistake, one that annoyed him. Mike found a message from Tac waiting for him when he arrived back at the flat. A rehearsal studio had been secured at short notice and would be available for the next two days. The band would be able to use the time to work on some of the new material that Tac had written. He wanted to start building on the live set, adding to it all the time.

A large part of the backline equipment would need unpacking, so that Tac could get at his guitars. It meant that Mike would have the ideal chance to give everything an overhaul before the next leg of the tour. A couple of Tac's guitars had been playing up during the previous dates. Although the problems were easy to address, it was still a time-consuming job. It wasn't something that Mike would want to do while on the road, if he could help it. He had managed to sort out some of the lesser issues, during the tour. Despite that, he knew there were other problems that would need a little more attention. Mike remembered that the studios had a large loading bay, car park and storage area behind them. That would be the ideal chance for him to unload the backline truck, so that it could have a much-needed service at the same time.

The two days after Mike Dean's meeting with Richard Levi, he was entombed in the dingy basement studio. He surrounded himself with Tac's guitars, effects pedals and racks of equipment. Working methodically, he made his way through cable looms and circuit boards. The whole place had the lingering smell of damp, which was far from ideal. Touching the walls, or what passed for a carpet, left Mike's fingers feeling sticky and unclean. He endured a constant fight against the urge to put anything down on the rotting carpet. It tried to cover the floor with its indefinable patterns but failed in many places. In the end, he bought a tarpaulin from a local hardware shop. At least with that under him, he felt more comfortable about putting things down, as he took each piece of equipment apart, bit by bit.

All the time he could hear the band as they continued working on the new numbers in the room next door. From where Mike was toiling away, he could tell that something about the sound had changed. What he heard coming through the badly soundproofed walls had a subtle new tone to it, a very different feel. The numbers they were working on seemed to be darker than those on the band's first album. That album had made up the majority of the live set so far, but Tac wanted to twist it into something new. The basic rhythm was now being set by the intense industrial beats that Tac was exploring. It gave the whole feel of the band much more intensity.

Mike Dean found it difficult to hear clearly from the side room where he laboured away. Despite that, the atmosphere of the sessions still managed to seep through to him. He could tell that the lyrics were different from the earlier ones, Tac had made a few comments about them and the diluted sounds confirmed that change. When Tac had shown him some of his initial ideas for new songs, the roughly sketched lyrics stood out. Mike couldn't help thinking that he had been reading far too much Aleister Crowley or Lovecraft, while he had been writing the new material.

When he arrived at the studio late on the second morning, Mike Dean found Tac sitting there on his own. He was playing away on his guitar; the rest of the band not having turned up yet. As they were chatting, Mike asked him about the new material. He mentioned the change in atmosphere and questioned what had taken his writing in that direction. Over the years, he had become interested in Tac's song writing processes and the things that inspired him, having had the idea of writing a biography at some time in the future. From what Tac told him, he hadn't realised that there had been any great change from the earlier songs. He hadn't thought about it in that way, he claimed. They were just things that came into his head, at one time or another, he went on to explain. Some things stuck there and worked out, others would disappear completely. Despite Tac's account, Mike had the feeling that he was unhappy talking about the lyrics that he had written. Shrugging them off as words, a vehicle for his guitar playing to roll with.

By the end of that second day, Mike Dean had Tac's equipment in full working order once again. With that job completed, he set about packing everything away, searching out their respective flight cases. When the backline truck arrived that afternoon, he had the job of fitting it all back inside. Everything was now ready for its return trip to the secure lock-up that they used. It would stay there until the tour restarted. With the afternoon now disappearing, the band's rehearsal time had come to an end, their two-day booking was up. They had only been able to book it at such short notice because another band had pulled out. That piece of luck gave them the chance to snap the time up. It was the reason that they were not working in their usual, far more lavish, rehearsal studios. That one was always booked solidly and needed arranging well in advance.

Everyone was happy to get the rehearsals out of the way. They now had a little over a week until they were due back out on the road again. It was well after nine o'clock by the time that Mike Dean managed to get home to find a note from Wendy. The note told him that she wouldn't be back until late, having had a last minute rush of things to deal with at work. A new line of t-shirts had arrived late in the day and had to be ready to send off that evening. Opening a bottle of red wine, Mike dropped a CD into the player and sat there thinking about what he would do the next day. It would be his first chance to go over to Hammersmith and pay a call on Toni Sillwood at the agency.

# Nine

Before he left the flat, late the next morning, Mike Dean phoned Richard at Levi's Books. He had been unable to reach him on his mobile after several attempts. Richard had a habit of letting his phone run out of charge, so it didn't surprise him. Plugging the phone in to recharge it seemed like an added complication to his life, one that he often forgot about. When Mike spoke to Jamie, he discovered that Richard wasn't around at that time. He had called in earlier to say that he would be back sometime in the afternoon but couldn't give an exact time. Leaving a message to explain what he was going do, Mike said that he would try to drop by the shop later. That would depend on how his meeting with Toni Sillwood went and whether he was able to find anything out. Straight afterwards, he left the same message on Richard's mobile, to be sure that he got it.

The agency consumed the whole floor of a large block of offices close to the centre of Hammersmith. Considering the area, Mike decided to take the tube through. That way he wouldn't have to fight with the London traffic or find somewhere to park. He knew that the trip from West Ham station would take the best part of an hour. That would give him plenty of time to decide on what he was going to say, when he met up with Toni Sillwood. Not having an appointment booked, he knew there was a chance that she wouldn't be there. He was taking a bit of a chance and might be wasting his time, but he was hoping to take her by surprise, if he could. Mike was hoping that not giving her any warning about his visit would put her on the back foot. With any luck, taken off guard, she would let something slip.

Mike Dean arrived at the agency a little before midday. The

moment he mentioned her name, the receptionist told him that Toni wasn't around at that time. She didn't take her eyes away from her computer screen for more than a few fleeting seconds as she spoke to him. Fighting for her attention, he pressed for information about Toni's movements for the day. In the end he was told that Toni was due back in the office within fifteen minutes to half an hour. That was if everything went to plan, the receptionist added unhelpfully. With her concentration returning to the screen in front of her, she switched away from Mike as if he wasn't there. Making his way down the stairs, Mike glanced at the posters that adorned the stairway walls. There was nowhere comfortable to wait in the cramped reception area and there had been no invitation to wait anyway.

The posters showed that the agency had been involved with an impressive range of acts over the years. They covered the whole spectrum of the music business. Mike found several posters for bands that he had worked with amongst the collection. There were a few names that surprised him, that he hadn't realised they had worked with. Once out in the street, Mike looked around and spotted The Swan, a pub that he hadn't been in for years, across the road from the offices. He decided to drop in for a drink, while he was waiting for Toni Sillwood to reappear. Mike was half-way through his pint of best bitter, when he glanced up to see Toni strolling through the door, her tall, athletic figure drawing looks from several people at the bar. She scanned the room as if she was trying to find someone. When she spotted Mike sitting there, she walked straight over to his table.

"Hi Mike, Sandy told me that you'd dropped by, asking for me." Toni Sillwood explained. As she spoke, she grabbed a badly printed and tatty looking menu from the table. "I'm starving, a workout always does that to me. Want anything to eat? The food's quite good in here, another drink?" Her words came out in a breathless stream as she dumped a packed kit bag onto the bench opposite Mike.

"Yeah, if you're buying, I'll have a veggie lasagne and another one of these." Mike Dean replied, pointing to the logo that adorned his glass.

"So, Mike, what can I do for you?" Toni Sillwood asked, when she returned to the table a few minutes later. Dropping her dark blue biker jacket onto the bench beside the kit bag, she slid into the seat opposite Mike. Glancing across the table, she waited for Mike to explain.

"Well, I know this is all going to sound a bit crazy, but… well, I… I was looking at a map of Europe the other day. Well, I couldn't help noticing that when you mark them out, the tour dates formed an almost perfect circle. When you add the new dates, they seem to mark out some kind of a star, it all seems rather odd, that's all." Mike Dean said, deciding to dive straight in with the facts, wanting to see what Toni's reaction might be.

"Ah, so you've noticed that, have you?" Toni Sillwood said, steepling her fingertips together in front of her. Her fore fingers rested on the bright red lipstick that highlighted her lips, as she stared across at Mike.

"I just thought that… well, there must be a reason for it. It couldn't have come out like that by chance, could it?"

"Yeah, I warned them that someone might pick up on that." Toni Sillwood added in an undertone, almost as she was talking to herself rather than to Mike.

"So, what's going on, Toni?" Mike Dean asked, watching her face for any signs of uneasiness or that she might be hiding something. She sat there twisting the silver nose ring, that stood out brightly against her warm dark skin. Other than that, there was no change in her reaction as far as Mike could see.

"Well, I'm working with a small group of people…" Toni Sillwood said, after a few minutes in thought, glancing around the room to see if anyone was paying them any attention. For a moment she looked uncomfortable about continuing. "Look, I shouldn't be telling you this at all, so please, keep it to yourself."

"Of course, Toni. It won't go any further."

"Well, Mike, you've come across pentagrams before, haven't you? Let's face it, they appear in thousands of tacky horror films. They often show links to the so-called left-hand path or black magic, if you prefer."

"Yeah, every goth in town seems covered in them now-a-days!"

"It's always been a powerful symbol." Toni Sillwood said, as their food arrived. A black-haired girl in leather, sporting a collection of pentagrams brought the dishes, as if to prove the point. "Well, it can also be a very powerful sign of protection, it can be used in very positive ways. The plan is to use this sign and seed the area with powerful talismans. We're hoping that by doing this we can generate a settled, far more stable influence across Europe."

"Well, I guess something needs doing." Mike Dean said, not really understanding a word of what he was hearing, it sounded like a fantasy story to him.

"All we're trying to do is negate some of the negativity that seems to be building up at this moment in time." Toni Sillwood explained, before taking a mouthful of her chips and adding. "I really shouldn't be eating these but, oh, they're so damned good. Guess that's an extra half hour in the gym tomorrow! I should know better, shouldn't I?"

Mike Dean wasn't sure what to say and instead he concentrated on his own meal. His head was spinning with ideas, as a tense silence settling between the two of them. To him, the whole thing sounded ridiculous, thinking about it, another question came into his mind.

"So, Toni, what you're telling me is that you're using the band to help you create this, this influence!" Mike Dean said, adding. "Does Tac know about this, or the rest of the band for that matter? Have you actually spoken to any of them about it?"

"No, Mike, Tac doesn't know anything… to, to be brutally honest, he doesn't need to know." Toni Sillwood said, staring into her half empty glass of mineral water. "The band needed a tour to promote the album, didn't they? The dates that I booked are pretty much the same as they would be without any of this going on. They just happen to be in a specific order. Okay, I agree there may be some strange gigs on the list but it's always good to try and break into new grounds. As an agent, I'm always looking for new opportunities, new venues for any of my acts."

By that time they had both finished their meals and were preparing to set off in their various directions. Toni Sillwood darted off back to her office, after taking a frantic call on her mobile. Apologising for having to rush off, she explained that she had an issue to deal with. By that time Mike Dean had the vague impression that she was making a little bit of sense. Alright, it was a bit strange, and she had gone about it in the wrong way, but there didn't appear to be any harm to it, as far as Mike could tell. If anything, there might be a positive outcome to it all. That was if the situation Toni had talked about worked, which he doubted. The whole matter sounded like something out of some tacky seventies' horror movie. He could see Peter Cushing saying the same type of thing to Christopher Lee.

During the conversation, Mike Dean asked Toni about Rick Fischer's involvement in the affair, wanting to know how he fitted into the project. Toni explained that she didn't know him very well, she had only met him a couple of times. She had first come across him through another member of her group. The woman who had made the introduction seemed to think that he was genuine, and they could trust him. Toni wasn't able to tell Mike much more about him, admitting that he was a bit of a mystery to her. She had heard that Rick had been part of a similar group to hers and had been with them for many years. Because of the recommendation, they decided that he would have an understanding of what was going on. They had checked him out and found nothing untoward. Rick had a background in tour management, having been out with several bands over the years. That meant he would be the ideal candidate to distribute their talismans.

Walking away from The Swan, Mike Dean headed back towards the nearest tube station. He was now feeling a little better, more positive than he had done since the end of the tour. Now he had a better feeling, he had something that helped to explain everything that he had seen. He could now take the information back to Richard Levi and see what he would make of it all. Until that day in Gothenburg, Mike had never thought about magic, black, white or any other colour. It was something from a work of fiction. A subject that belonged in the books that he could remember reading as a teenager. Now it looked as if it was not only real but widespread, he couldn't help feeling a little bemused by the whole situation that he found himself in.

Toni Sillwood and her group appeared to have the best of intentions, they seemed to be working for the common good. That was if he could believe everything that she had told him, and he had the impression that she was genuine. The one issue that still troubled him was the covert way that the operation had run, that didn't sit right to him. If there was nothing wrong with what they were doing, why not come out and shout about it? They could tell people, especially the band, as they were unwitting accomplices in it all. At least, Toni had been able to allay the worst of Mike Dean's fears. Although whether Richard would agree with his take on what he had learnt, only time would tell.

Making his way to the tube station, Mike Dean set out towards Camden and Levi's Books. He was aware of a relaxed feeling about everything taking over, causing him to feel more comfortable. He had set out to find answers to the questions that were rolling around in the back of his head, now he was returning with some explanations. Whether they would hold up to closer scrutiny, only time would tell. Arriving at Levi's Books, Mike found that Richard had still not put in an appearance and hadn't been in contact. Jamie, his assistant, explained that he hadn't been around for a couple of days. He had disappeared with little notice, soon after his last meeting with Mike. All that he had told Jamie, before he ran off, was that he had some matters to look into. It wasn't unusual for him to run off for days or weeks on end like that, it was something that Jamie had become used to.

It was perfectly normal for Richard to disappear for days at a time. He would often be off attempting to track down rare editions of books that he wanted. Sometimes he would be out there searching for items that he'd heard rumours about, trying to find the facts. Richard had several regular customers who were always looking for obscure books, asking about their availability and sending him on a mission to locate them. Tracking them down could take time but as he often claimed, the rewards were worth it. Making a cup of coffee, Jamie said that Richard had been acting as if he had become preoccupied by something, getting more clumsy than usual by the day. It was always a tell-tale sign that he was going to rush off on a mad mission. Over the few days before his latest disappearance, his awkwardness had turned worse than ever. It was as if his mind had become focused on something else, capturing his attention. Mike was about to give up and make the trip home, when Richard reappeared in a flurry of activity.

"Hey, Mike, how's it going?" Richard Levi asked, darting straight through the shop and into the office at the back. As he passed, he beckoned for Mike to follow him. "I got your message, was about to give you a call. Been a bit tied up with things. Have you had a chance to meet up with Toni Sillwood yet?"

"Yeah, I met up with her earlier." Mike said, adding. "I had quite a long chat with her, it was quite illuminating! That's why I thought that I'd come over."

"Ah, this should be rather interesting." Richard Levi said, an intense expression crossing his face. "So, Mike, did she have anything interesting to say about all this?"

Clearing a seat, Mike Dean ran though the conversation he'd had with Toni Sillwood. He told Richard everything that she had said regarding the matter. He explained what she had said about the talismans and how Rick Fischer fitted into the project. Mike continued with his account by explaining how Rick planned to distribute the talismans at specific points. As he related the information about what Toni was hoping to gain from the whole adventure, he wondered if it made any sense. Richard listened to everything that Mike told him in silence. He jotted down some odd notes on a large pad that sat on the table in front of him but said nothing. Once Mike had finished his account, Richard jumped to his feet. He was close to knocking the table over as he strode up and down the room in a world of his own. Tapping his thumb against his forehead and mumbling to himself, he appeared troubled. After a few minutes, he came to some form of decision, returning to where Mike was sitting, he perched on the edge of the closest table.

"This does fit with some of the things that I've managed to find out over the last few days." Richard Levi said. His tone of voice and the deep frown on his face made it look as if he was unconvinced by the story that he had heard.

"You don't sound too certain…" Mike Dean noted.

"Well… I, I've found out about a group based in the UK. They have quite heavy Druidic links, calling themselves The Union of the Mountain Ash."

"Never head of them myself." Mike Dean said, feeling a little amused by the name but trying not to show it.

"No… no, nor had I until the other day. They're quite a secretive bunch, which always seems to be the way with these people!" Richard Levi said. "They profess to be using magical influences to stabilise, not only Europe, but the whole of the world."

"Definitely sounds like it could be the group that Toni was

telling me about."

"Yeah, I guess so, their aims and ways of working seem to be the same." Richard Levi said, although without any conviction.

"So, we've got nothing to worry about then, this has all been a bit of a false alarm." Mike Dean said, taking a deep breath in relief before adding. "Or, is there something else that you've found out, something that you haven't told me yet?"

"Oh, I'm not really certain about anything at the moment, Mike." Richard Levi replied. "Let's not start jumping to premature conclusions." Springing to his feet once again, he crossed to one of his book cabinets. Pulling out two large volumes with ornate leather covers, he placed them on the table. He had cleared the space in his usual manner by pushing his notebook and pieces of paper onto the floor. Opening the first book to a page that he had marked with a torn strip of card, he spread it out on the table.

"So, you still think that there's something wrong with all this?" Mike Dean asked.

"The things that Toni's told you do make some sense, I'll admit that." Richard Levi said, as he ran his finger down the page in front of him. "But, I think we should look a bit closer at the meanings behind those symbols that you saw on those bricks."

"So, what are you looking for, Rich?"

"I'm not sure, at the moment, to be honest. Ah, now, if the bricks that were being used were those with the symbol for noun, as I suggested before. Well, then I would tend to agree with you. There's every reason to believe that they could be a good influence on things. Especially if they're distributed as you've said they are."

"Okay, so, what's the other option?"

"Well, my problem with all this starts with the black candles and the smell that you described coming from them. That makes me think about it all a little differently." Richard Levi explained.

"Yeah, I hadn't thought about them. The smell was awful, it was almost like rotting meat!" Mike Dean said, remembering the scent that had drifted around the graveyard. The memory on its own made him come over a little unwell.

"And the bricks that were actually used had the other symbol on them, those with aein etched into them. That sign seems to give a far darker, more negative swing to the whole situation." Richard Levi said, closing the book with a deft flick and opening the next one in the pile. "Used in this way, it's more likely to lead towards instability and chaos than anything else."

"I've got to say that Toni gave me no reason to believe that she had anything but the best of intentions." Mike Dean stated. "There was no hint at anything darker going on, no… no evil trends."

"It's strange you should use that word, Mike." Richard Levi said in an undertone. Closing the book that he'd been looking through, he stared at Mike intensely. "I can't shake the idea that what you've stumbled on here is something that can best be described by that one word… evil. The question is, what are we going to do about it?"

"Well, is it possible that Rick Fischer is working for some other organisation? Some kind of double agent?" Mike Dean asked, adding. "That he's deliberately putting out the wrong talismans."

"Yeah, I must admit that I've thought about that too, it's a definite possibility." Richard Levi said, after a few moments, he added. "I don't think we can take the chance of confronting Toni

Sillwood with any of this, not yet anyway. There's always a chance that she knows exactly what's going on."

"Well, I guess so." Mike Dean replied. "Although, I must say that I didn't get that impression from her."

"Mike, we can't afford to be too careful here. When's the tour due to start up again?"

"End of next week, we start over here in Leeds and Norwich, then we're off for Germany." Mike Dean said, glancing at the list in front of him, to be certain of the schedule.

"Well, at least that gives us a little bit of leeway, a bit of time to play with." Richard Levi claimed. "I'm going to see what I can find out about this group and any others that might be out there, for good or bad."

"Anything I can do to help?"

"No. not really, at least, not at the moment, Mike. If I don't get back to you before the tour starts up again, you'll have to keep a close eye on Rick Fischer."

"This is all starting to get a bit out of my league." Mike Dean said, wondering what he had managed to get himself mixed up with. "You make it all sound so normal, as if the use of magic is an everyday occurrence. Like Harry Potter or something. I keep having to pinch myself to check that I'm not actually dreaming any of this."

"Oh no, Mike. Don't make that mistake, this is definitely not a dream." Richard Levi said. "If this is all leaning in the direction that it seems to be. Well, you might be justified in calling it a nightmare but even that wouldn't disguise the truth of the matter. This has definitely got the potential of being evil."

# Ten

"I can see her now!

"Yeah, just recently I've been able to actually fucking see her, all dressed up in her dull white gown. It's a gown that's a little bit like the old man's one, but hers is a strange off-white in colour. In fact, there's almost no colour to it at all, if that makes any sense.

"Course she's not entirely visible. It's a bit like looking at a thin white cloud, hanging there in the air, but one that's in the rough shape of a woman, bit like a… a ghost, I suppose.

"Ha! I'm being haunted! What do you think of that then?

"She's standing there staring at me from the corner of the room at this moment. That damned witchy woman, see, I've been telling you she was a woman all along, haven't I?

"There's always this rigid expression stuck on her damned face. It comes with this aura of intense disapproval. I can't help feeling that she's disgusted with me and what I'm doing.

"I've got to see this whole thing through though, whatever she thinks about it. I can't let her get in my way, can't let her stop me now. Anyway, she ain't physical, is she? How's she gonna stop me?

"Something else that's a little bit strange, I can see that her lips are always moving too. It's as if she's trying to tell me something, trying to communicate with me. I can't hear a damned word though, well, there is a faint buzzing noise in the background. It's a bit like a swarm of bees in the back of the room, but there's nothing else.

"I wish I could work out who she is, what she's after, why she's bugging me like this. What have I done to upset her? If I found the answers to those questions, maybe I could find a way to stop her from bothering me.

"I can't work out whether she's for real or just an apparition of some type, a, a ghost if you like! Oh, I don't know. What do I do? I've never had to deal with anything of this kind before.

"I performed another of those rituals last night. It was a new one that I found it in the old man's books. This one was called a true name ritual. Course, I tweaked it a little bit, added my own touch to it, wanted to try and get a bit more out of it.

"It was something that came to me completely out of the blue, happened when I put that gown on again. At that moment I had this idea of how I could expand the whole thing, make it work better for me.

"You see, the book told me that if I could find someone's true name, then I could hold some power over them. I'd have a way of being able to control them. Course, I had the idea that if I could find her real name like that, then I would be able to control her. I could get her off me back, once and for all.

"It was about half hour after I'd performed that ritual for the first time, once I had everything cleared up. I was wondering whether I'd see any signs of success or would she just disappear.

"I was sitting in the kitchen, trying to decide what to do next, when I heard it for the first time. It was some kind of voice-like thing that came to me but it wasn't a normal kinda voice. Sounded like there was dozens of voices, all coming at me at once, all sitting on top of each other. It was like some bizarre psychedelic choir.

"However much I tried, I was unable to focus on any single

one of them voices. They all seemed to be saying the same thing, but I couldn't tell what they was trying to say to me.

"I was pretty damned sure they was trying to communicate with me, though. They was trying to tell me something.

"I'm setting everything up ready to perform a new ritual now. See, I'm getting confident with all this, I'm starting to get good at it.

"Got the idea when I read something in an old leaflet, it was stained and fragile but I could read it, just. I found it stuck inside the cover on one of the old man's books. It mentioned some bloke called John Dee; never heard of him before.

"See, I've finally managed to do it. I've plucked up the courage to look at the old man's bedroom. Go through a few of the things that I found in there. There was a collection of books on the shelf in there. Some of them was quite interesting ones too. They was all things he obviously wanted to keep nearby. Didn't want them with the rest of the stuff, stuck away in that suitcase or on the bookcase downstairs.

"That leaflet I found, stuck inside the cover of that book, mentioned the forty-nine keys. It said how you could use them to bring the destruction of the world with the raising of the antichrist.

"Antichrist? Yeah, that's what it said, course I know that's all bollocks! I know it's all crap, but the basics of the ritual could be useful, if I can use it properly.

"Problem with many of these leaflets, they was written a long time ago. The language is a bit screwy, have to try and decipher it, work out what it's saying. I need to look at all those so-called keys. The one I really want to look at, well, that's the first one, the one that's not to be opened. Yeah, that's what it says! It's not to be opened, cos it's too sacred and mysterious.

"Yeah? Well, that sounds just like my kinda thing, don't it? See, to my mind there's gotta be a reason for something like that. If they want to hide things, keep people away from them, then they should say, here it is, look at it. No one would take any notice of it then, say you can't do it and the whole world wants to, or is that just me?

"Really gonna have to go through all those books again. See if I can find a ritual to dispel that damned witchy woman. I'm sure there must be something like that in there somewhere.

"Maybe I could make one up myself, if I can't find one that's any good. I'm sure the gown would be able to help me with that.

"She seems to be there pretty much all the time now; bugging me, haunting me, getting on my damned nerves. She was standing there in the doorway earlier when I saw her. At first it was just a faint glow as usual but I could tell it was her, even though I could see straight through her.

"What did I do? I'll tell you what I did, I walked straight through her and out the damned door, that's what I did. Didn't try to stop me, don't think she could have if she wanted to, but fuck it was cold as I went through. Chilled me to the bone that did; don't think I'll try to do that again. Even makes me feel cold talking about it.

"A ritual to fuck off a spirit? Yeah, that's what I need.

"Maybe, if I brought the old man back, I could talk to him about it, would he be able to tell me any more about her. He did warn me that she would follow me, after all, didn't he?

"Sure I've read something about bringing people back. Seeing as he mentioned her in that letter he left me, he must know more about her. He said she'd haunt me, well, she's fucking doing that all right, ain't she? He might even be able to tell me how to get rid of her.

"Shit! I couldn't face that though, not having to talk to him. I'll have to find it for myself. I really need to discover who she is first, that's important, that is. Only then will I be able to find any clues on how to stop her.

"Gotta say this John Dee fella was a clever bloke, he's got some good stuff here. He says he spent a lot of time trying to talk to what he calls angels, so he could learn things.

"Don't think they was angels though, think they was something totally different.

"Prapse I could tap into that myself! Could I find a way of talking to them so called angels. Wonder what they'd be able to tell me.

"Language is all a bit oldy English, all a bit odd, but this gown seems to understand it. I'm sure it's trying to help me with this.

"Think I'm gonna try and make my own dark mirror, like the one he had. That could prove to be useful, that could. If I can do it.

"Ha! I'm sure I can, I can do anything I wanna do. He had one made from obsidian, had to look that one up on the web, never heard of it before. Found out its some kinda volcanic glass, but I'm sure I would be able to use something a little bit easier to get hold of though.

"Prapse an old junk shop mirror could do it, I'm sure, if I work it right. Have to think about that one.

"It's not what you've got, it's how you use it that's important, ain't it?

"From what I can see, a ritual performed with a dark mirror under candlelight is the way to go. If I do it right, it will show the reflections of any hidden entities that might be floating around. Hopefully, if it works, that way at least I'll have a good look at her, find out what I'm dealing with.

"There is a little a warning that I found about it though. Says if I can see them, then they would be able to see me too.

"Yeah? Well, what they gonna do to me then? They can bring it on if they think they can! I'll take them all on, ain't scared of them fuckers."

# Eleven

The band had been on the road for several weeks, travelling up and down the motorways of Europe. Now the second leg of The Demon Eaters European tour was drawing to a close. The whole tour had proven to be a very successful series of gigs. It felt as if it had taken ages, but at last, they found themselves making their way towards Belgium. The final gig of the tour would be at Magasin 4 in Brussels. From Brussels, they would be heading home for a well-earned rest; the series of dates had been an intense one with few days off. The second leg had been far more successful than the first one had been. They had seen packed crowds and a massive upturn in sales of their t-shirts, CDs and other merchandise. It was clear to everybody that the word was out about the band, at last. That was due in part to several high-profile interviews and radio spots that they had done.

The band now found themselves on the front covers of the music press and websites across Europe. They had heard that the coverage was reaching America too and the reactions over there had been good. Tac had become a bit of a celebrity as the tour rolled on, his face appearing in every town that they visited. Mike Dean managed to keep a tight an eye on Rick Fischer's movements during those weeks on the road. He continued to act in exactly the same way as he had done before. At least it told Mike, that he was unaware that his actions were on their radar. Whenever he noticed him disappearing, Mike made a note of the time and place. Every few days he would phone Richard Levi to update him on what was going on.

During the first week of the tour, Rick Fischer slipped away from the venue in Hamburg, as he had done before. Mike Dean took that opportunity to take another look in Rick's locker, while the tour coach was empty. On that occasion, he found that Rick was well-prepared for his distribution process. This time he had two identical flight cases stashed away in his locker. The first one of them, that Mike looked at, was brand new. On opening it, he found that its contents were intact, none of the bricks were missing. That case contained two full sets all vacuum sealed in cellophane. The top layer had a new symbol etched on them. Looking at the new symbol, Mike felt that it was like the letter G, although a rather stylised one. The bottom layer of bricks had the sign they believed to be that of noun.

Later that afternoon Mike Dean managed to find time to phone Richard Levi. The gap in his routine came between the soundcheck and the doors to the venue opening to let the expectant crowds in. Mike wanted to tell him about his latest findings and especially the new bricks that he had uncovered. The moment he spoke to Richard, he launched straight into describing the symbol that he'd seen etched on the bricks. As soon as he mentioned the new symbol, Richard wanted to hear more about it. He asked several questions, trying to get as good a description as possible and its alignment to the edges. Mike continued, telling him about the bricks that he had found in the second of the cases. The top layer being those marked with the symbol for aein, several of which were missing. The other bricks held a figure that Mike could only describe as an ornate Q. He explained that there were two spaces in that layer, where bricks had once sat.

Richard asked some other questions relating to the things that Mike Dean had discovered. He was interested to hear more about Rick Fischer's general behaviour during the tour. He wanted to know if it had changed at all and how he was reacting to the people that he met. After talking for ten minutes, Mike suddenly found himself surrounded by people. The support band were bustling around in the backstage area, busy tuning guitars and getting themselves ready to take to the stage. Finding that he was becoming distracted by the activity, Mike said that he would have to go. The whole area was now far too noisy and congested for them to continue talking. Before finishing the call, he said that he would be in contact again as soon as possible.

Another two days were to pass by as the tour rolled on before Mike Dean had the chance to talk to Richard Levi. On that occasion it took several attempts for him to get through. He found that Richard had been busy during that time, and there was a lot of information that he wanted to run over. The new symbols that Mike had described were those of phe and samekh, Richard explained. That was if they kept to the Cabbalistic theme that he had established as being the most probable link. The sign for phé, Richard said, stood for the tarot card of The Star. The other one, the symbol for samekh, stood for The Devil.

From his investigations, the situation now looked clear to him. He was certain that Rick Fischer had managed to infiltrated Toni Sillwood's group for some unknown reason. It was either for his own purposes or for those of a rival organisation. He still couldn't be sure whether Rick was working alone or not. There had to be a high chance that he was in league with some other group, Richard claimed. Whatever it was that he was doing, he was working against everything that the union were trying to do, that was for sure. The talismans that the union would use to pursue their goal where the ones that bore the marks of noun and phé. These signs, Richard explained, stood for liberation and the harmony of thought. Rick Fischer was using completely different ones, those with aein and samekh on them, which stood for division and the destructive urges.

The tour carried on, its usual routines taking hold and pushing them forward. The whole process was running like a well-oiled machine, most of the time. Mike Dean kept a watch on Rick Fischer as he continued disappearing and reappearing. He was acting as secretively as on the first leg of the tour, his case of talismans becoming lighter by the day. During that time Mike spoke to Richard Levi as often as he was able to. Trying to keep him updated on everything that was going on, especially with Rick. After a long discussion, they had decided that following Rick again would not be a good idea. It might make it all far more difficult, if he realised the surveillance was going on. They didn't want to take the chance of spooking him and having him do something to react against them.

One evening, as they reached the last week of the tour, Richard Levi called. He informed Mike Dean that he had been able to make contact with someone on the inside of The Union of the Mountain Ash. That meeting had confirmed that his worst fears had come true. This new contact was quite high up in the inner circle of The Union, he explained. It soon became clear that he had nothing to do with the talismans that Rick was distributing. After hearing about the new development, he was quite disturbed by the disruption. Richard said that he was now trying to arrange a meeting with the inner circle of the union. That was proving to be far more difficult than he would have hoped it to be though.

As the tour continued, Mike Dean had been noticing that there were a few slow changes coming over Tac. Some of them were things that he had to admit he found a little unsettling. The changes were subtle, and he was aware that most people wouldn't think anything more about them. Having worked alongside Tac for so many years, they stood out like a sore thumb to Mike. One of the more obvious things that jumped out was that Tac now wore black clothes, almost all the time. His old glitzy persona of silks and scarves, with its glam rock edge having completely gone. Of course, Mike realised that it could all be to do with the new style of music that he was performing. The old glam sounds of his previous bands were now very much a thing of the past.

Another thing that Mike found troubling was that Tac had now become far more withdrawn. It had now come to such a state that he hardly spoke to anyone anymore. He rarely spoke, even to Mike, unless he had no choice or circumstances made it impossible to avoid. It was only when all the small changes came together that Mike noticed them clearly. With those on his mind, he began to realise the result that they were having on his friend. He was sure that it would shock Sam, if she saw the state that he was now in. Not having seen him for several weeks, the changes would leap out at her. She had picked up on the few little changes that had happened during the first leg of the tour. Now those changes would be far more obvious to her.

The final proof that everything was not as it should be, didn't come until the tour had ended. The band and crew made it back to London in the early afternoon, after the ferry crossing and drive home. Once the equipment was secure in their lock-up, they all parted company, everyone disappearing in their own separate directions. Mike Dean found himself sitting at home on that first evening back, Wendy having met up with a group of old friends. He was feeling exhausted, after the drive and helping stack the band's equipment away. Their storage facility was always the first stop the moment that they returned to London. The hire trucks were all due out again within a few days, leaving little change over time, they needed cleaning and preparing for the next band.

Wendy was out for the evening with some old college friends, leaving Mike to his own devices. He had been planning on sitting in front of the television for the night. If he could stay awake, he was hoping that watching Arsenal take on Spurs and with luck beat them, would keep him amused for a couple of hours. It was some time since he'd had the chance to watch his favourite team in action. A few minutes after the match had kicked off, Mike's evening took a turn for the worse. The frantic ringing of the doorbell forced him to his feet. Swearing under his breath, Mike got up and put his can of larger onto the table. Heading towards the front door, he took a deep breath before opening it, unsure of what he might find. The moment that he saw the expression on Sam's face, he knew that something was wrong.

"Oh, thank god you're in! Can we come in?" Sam asked, wiping tears away from her face with the back of her hand. Not waiting for an answer, she guided Cheyenne's pushchair through into the lounge.

The moment that Cheyenne had escaped the confines of her pushchair, she was off and running. She made her way towards the bedroom shouting. "Me go find Teddy."

Wendy had a giant panda that stood in the corner of the bedroom and Cheyenne knew exactly where to find it. It was always one of her first ports of call, whenever she came around to the flat. The bear was as large as Cheyenne was and after wrestling with it, she would often fall asleep laying on top of it. With the room to themselves for a moment, Mike asked what had happened to cause Sam to be in such a state. In normal circumstances she was always one of the most calm and steady people, even in a crisis.

"It's Tac…" Sam said, although Mike had guessed that much. Perching on the edge of the sofa, she dabbed at the corner of her eyes with a handkerchief as she spoke.

"Yeah, I kind of guessed that it might be." Mike replied.

"There's definitely something wrong with him, although he refuses to accept it. He says that everything's fine!" Sam whispered, as Cheyenne returned to the lounge dragging the panda behind her. She dropped down with it next to the beanbag that sat in front of the coffee table and began talking to it.

"So, what's going on?" Mike asked, switching the television over from the football. Finding some cartoon programmes, he turned up the volume a little to help obscure their voices.

"Oh, I don't know, Mike! He's just not the same person that he was before the tour. He's changed over those weeks." Sam said, trying to explain the changes that she had found in him. "Are you sure he's not back on the gear, Mike?"

"Well, I'm as sure as I can be. I've seen no signs of anything like that going on." Mike replied honestly, convinced that he was right on that score.

"Well, something's going on, Mike." Sam said, trying to hold back the tears that were threatening to overwhelm her once more. "Have you noticed anything?"

"I have noticed that he's been keeping his distance from everyone, but that can often happen on a tour, as you know."

"Yeah, I know, I've seen that happen before."

"And don't forget, he's never been in the position of having his name on the posters, in all the media. I kind of guessed it was something to do with that. The pressure getting to him." Mike Dean explained.

"Is there nothing else you can tell me?" Sam asked.

"I'm sorry, Sam. I saw some small changes, I'll admit that. Don't forget I'm working with him day after day, it's difficult to see how serious any changes might be. At the end of the day, I'm just too close to him."

Sam explained how everything had come to a head earlier that evening. Tac had turned on her for no reason, something that he had never done before. At the time he had been telling her about his plan to head out to Germany for a break. With the tour over, he said that he wanted some down time. Sam believed that the trip he was planning would be for the three of them, as would usually be the case at the end of a tour. It had always been a way for the three of them to reconnect after having been apart for months. The moment that she had asked where they were going, Tac had snapped and lost the plot.

He began shouting at her, shouting about wanting to go away on his own, somewhere that he could have space from people. Sam had become upset by his unexpected reaction. Asking for some explanation to the change of routine, he turned around and slapped her across the face. That was something that he had never done before, even in his most out of control moments. The blow hadn't been a hard one, but the shock of it was like a hammer blow to Sam. She couldn't believe that he could do anything like that. The instant that he did it, Tac realised what he had done. He began mumbling vague apologies, but he was talking in a whispered undertone making it hard to hear. When Cheyenne ran into the kitchen to find out what was going on, Tac recoiled and moved away. After a moment in thought, he turned round and stormed out of the house.

At first Sam was so shocked by the whole episode that she didn't know what to do. Standing there in the kitchen, she stared at the door that was still shaking in its frame. Her mind was reeling with conflicting thoughts. As the silence of the house settled in around her, it seemed to be squeezing the breath out of her. The atmosphere was broken by Cheyenne's questioning about what had happened. After a few moments, Sam managed to spur herself into action, she couldn't stand there doing nothing. Her first idea was to search through a large pile of papers that stood on the computer desk in the lounge. Amongst them she found a single airline ticket to Hannover. It was sitting on top of a selection of concert flyers and other documents.

That discovery was enough to tell Sam that Tac had always been planning on going on the trip alone. There had never been any intention of taking her and Cheyenne with him. That idea had triggered another unwanted thought in the back of Sam's mind, was Tac seeing another woman in Germany? Mike Dean managed to allay her fears on that score; he was certain that there was nothing like that going on. He was sure that he would have noticed and anyway, there hadn't been the time. The shows had come back-to-back, with few breaks in the packed schedule. As they continued talking, they ran over everything that had happened during the tour. Cheyenne curled up on the beanbag in front of the television and fell asleep after a short time.

Later that evening, Wendy returned from her night out. It took one look at Sam's face to tell her that something had happened. She guessed straight away that it had to be to do with Tac in some way. Retreating to the kitchen where they could talk, Wendy said that they would have to stay for the night. While they were talking, Mike prepared the spare room for their stay. At first Sam insisted that she would have to get back. She wanted to be there when Tac returned but she said that she would leave Cheyenne with them, as she was asleep. It didn't take long, considering the state that Tac had been in, for Wendy to convince her not to go back that night. Mike saying that he would take them, the next morning, to make sure that everything was okay.

Mike Dean was hoping that once Tac had spent a night on his own, he would change tact. Having the time to think through everything, would hopefully go some way to settling whatever was going on in his head. Before carrying Cheyenne off to the bedroom, he asked about the date on the ticket to Germany. He wanted to find out when it had been booked for, as he was hoping to establish some kind of a timeline. Unfortunately, Sam was unable to give him the details that he was after. She had been so shocked by what had happened and finding the ticket that nothing had sunk in. With everything on her mind, she hadn't been able to take in any of the details. It had been more than enough to find that the ticket had been for Tac and not the three of them.

Sometime later, before she went off to join Cheyenne in the spare room, Sam tried to call Tac. Finding that his phone went straight through to his answer phone message, she guessed that it had been switched off. She left a message to explain where she and Cheyenne were, although she was pretty sure that he would have guessed. She didn't want to disappear for the night without saying anything.

# Twelve

After Mike Dean had eaten a light breakfast, he took time to play some games on his laptop with Cheyenne. By eleven o'clock, Sam was eager to make a move and suggested that they should be heading home. Packing Sam and Cheyenne into the car, Mike drove them through the London traffic, to take them back. He could tell that Sam was still worried about what she might find, although she was trying hard not to show it. She was determined to keep it to herself, not wanting to worry Cheyenne. Sam had called Tac that morning but his phone went straight into the answer phone, as it had the previous night. As Mike had offered his services in accompanying them, she was more than happy to take him up on it. If Tac was in a rough way, she knew that if anyone, Mike would be the one that would be able to reason with him.

The moment that they reached the front door and Sam slid her key into the lock, she told Mike that Tac wasn't there. She couldn't explain how she knew it, but she was clear to her before she stepped through the door. The first thing that she did, once they entered the house, was to rush straight up the stairs to their bedroom. Sam could tell that Tac had spent the night there by the unmade bed and general clutter in the room. Obviously he had decided to go out earlier that morning. Was his absence designed to make sure that he missed their return, Sam wondered. To her relief, Sam noticed that his travelling bags were still standing in the corner of the room. At least that told her that he hadn't left the country yet.

Making her way back to the ground floor, Sam headed through to the lounge. The plane ticket was still laying on top of the pile of papers where she had dropped it the previous night. Studying the ticket closely, for the first time, she saw that the flight was due at three o'clock the following afternoon. At least that would give them time to talk about things before he left, she told herself. With Sam running around the house looking for signs of what Tac had been up to, Mike Dean turned to Cheyenne. Helping her off with her coat, he followed her through to her room to hang it up for her. She was more than happy to be back home again amongst her toys, it was a place where she felt safe. Picking up a doll from the floor, she made her way over to Mike to show him.

"Where's Daddy, Uncle Mike?" She asked, aware that Tac wasn't around. When he was home, he would always come straight to her. "Fink he's not vewy well. He didn't say night night to me last night." She added.

"He's going to be fine, Baby." Mike Dean said, hoping that he was in fact telling her the truth. "Why not go and play with Mandy while I help Mummy."

"She's not Mandy!" Cheyenne said in a voice that told Mike Dean that he should have known better. "She's Jane." She added, before running off towards her toy cupboard.

When Mike Dean managed to find Sam, she was standing beside the sink in the kitchen. Looking out of the window, as clouds blew across the otherwise deep blue sky, she had a lost expression on her face. Mike could see a large sheet of paper clasped in her hands. Hearing him enter the kitchen, she handed the note over, so that he could read it. She explained that she had found it attached to the front of the fridge. It had been placed there with one of the collection of large guitar shaped magnets that were there. The unmistakable handwriting was an untidy scrawl, nothing unusual for Tac. Mike had become used to deciphering his hieroglyphics over the years.

The note said that he was sorry for having lost his temper and hitting her. He when on to explain that he needed some time to himself, after the pressure of the tour, it would be a way for him to clear his head. The reasoning behind his decision to run off alone was that the pressures of the tour had managed to get on top of him. He hadn't realised how hard it would be with everything focused on him, he went on to explain. At the end of the note, Tac said that he would be leaving the next afternoon. He went on to suggest that Sam and Cheyenne should join him in Hannover, once he'd had time to pull himself together. The whole tone of the note was much more like the Tac that they both knew. Mike could see that Sam was feeling a little more relaxed, after having read it, her previous tension having eased.

Mike Dean waited until he was sure that Sam was going to be alright, that the events of the previous evening had eased. Once he was happy with the situation, he said his goodbyes and rushed off, explaining that he had a lot to do. With everything that had been going on, he felt that he needed to meet Richard Levi as soon as possible. He wanted to update him with all the latest information. The trip through the busy early afternoon traffic into Camden Town, proved to be a hectic one. After driving around, Mike managed to find a parking space that was not too far away from the bookshop.

Richard poured a large measure of his favourite whiskey, something that he would do at any time of the night or day. Mike ran through everything that had happened between Tac and Sam, the previous evening. Coming to the end of his account, he had to ask whether Richard thought it had any bearing on the what they had discovered themselves. As he spoke, Mike Dean watched Richard Levi's face turn slightly pale. His expression solidifying into a taunt mask, as he told him about the events of the previous night. The moment that he had finished speaking, Richard was on his feet and darting around the office. Flicking open odd books and files from various cabinets, he became a whirlwind of activity. After a few minutes of manic searching, he had several pieces of paper clutched in his hand. There was someone that he needed to meet up with, he announced, heading towards the office door.

As he left the bookshop, he almost collided with a customer who was coming in through the main door. Out on the street, he asked Mike if he would be able to return the following afternoon, before rushing away. Moments later he had disappeared off up the street, fading into the distance. His parting words were that there wasn't anything more he could say, at that time. Once he had spoken to whoever it was that he was going off to meet, he hoped to have more to say.

* * *

When he returned to Levi's Books early on that Wednesday afternoon, Mike Dean was feeling hot and sweaty. He had negotiated the swarming lunchtime crowds of Camden but it had been stressful. The moment that he entered the shop, he found himself being ushered through to Richard's office once again. It came as quite a surprise to find Toni Sillwood sitting in the cluttered back room. As Mike closed the door behind him, Toni was deep in conversation with Richard Levi. Walking through the stacks of books, he cleared a chair to enable him to sit down. He tried to relax, not wanting to disturb the two of them, until Toni rose to her feet and turned towards him, with her hand out. A taunt smile crossed her face, highlighted by her usual bright red lipstick. It was the only makeup that she ever seemed to wear; it complimented her deep brown skin to perfection.

"Mike, it's good to see you again." She said, shaking Mike Dean's hand in a firm grip. "I must thank you for bringing this whole matter to our attention. If you hadn't been so vigilant, hadn't spotted all this going on, well, who knows what might have happened."

"Well, come on then, Toni. What is going on, do you know?" Mike Dean asked, hoping that he would get some answers.

"I will explain things in a moment, the best that I can, anyway." She said, twisting her nose ring in a nervous movement that Mike had noticed before. It left him with the feeling that something unanticipated was about to follow. "Before I go any further though, I've got to ask you if you'd be willing to travel out to Germany with us… tomorrow?"

"Tomorrow!" Mike gasped, taken aback by the suddenness of the idea. "Well… I, I guess so, if you think you need me to."

"It would be good if you're able to, Mike. We could well need your help out there."

"It's a bit short notice! Wendy's going to be a bit pissed off, but I'm sure I can do it, if I have to."

"I hoped you'd agree, Mike. In fact, I've already booked the tickets, bit premature I know, but I was confident that you'd agree to come. We're booked on the four o'clock flight, tomorrow afternoon, if that's okay with you."

"Yeah, I, I suppose so…"

"The other day, when I spoke to you, I told you about the

group that I've been working with." Toni Sillwood went on to say. Gesturing for Mike to take the seat that he had cleared and was now standing beside the desk.

"Yeah, got to say that it all sounded a bit odd. The more I've thought about it, Toni, the more I'm not sure how much sense any of it made."

"Well, as Richard has already told you, The Union of the Mountain Ash is an organisation with Druidic links. Our aims are to promote peace throughout Europe and the world at large. We're trying to do this through the use of complimentary magic."

"That's pretty much what Richard's already told me, Toni."

"Well, what you seem to have uncovered on this tour is a group who are attempting to undermine our work."

"So, you think that this is all some other group of people, Toni?"

"Can't be sure about that, at the moment, Mike. It could just be Rick Fischer working on his own, but that does seem a little unlikely. Well, whoever they are, they're using reactive magical influences for their own purposes. Rick seems to be right at the centre of it all." Toni Sillwood explained.

"This all sounds pretty unreal…"

"I realise that this might all sound a little strange, Mike. Especially to someone largely unaware of the magical influences. I've got to admit that we're all quite shocked by the things that have been going on."

"So, do you think that Rick is working with other people, or on his own?" Mike Dean asked.

"Oh, I'm sure Rick must be working with others! I can't see

him doing it himself. Somehow, he's been able to infiltrate the outer circle of the organisation." Richard Levi said, before Toni Sillwood could answer the question. "It seems clear that he's been using the tour to distribute his own destabilising objects. From what you've seen, he hasn't touched the ones that were given to him."

"That's right, Rich." Toni said, with a slight nod of her head. "There's one other thing that I was about to tell you, just before Mike arrived."

"Anything interesting, Toni?"

"Well, since I spoke to you yesterday, we've been able to find out something about him. Rick Fischer is quite a high up member of a group based in Germany. They call themselves The Star of Destiny, would you believe?"

"Never heard of them." Richard Levi stated. "At least not outside some of the old paperback thrillers that are laying around the shop. Sounds like something out of The Man from Uncle!"

"Yeah, I know what you mean, I guess it's something that's got a bit lost in translation." Toni Sillwood said, before continuing to relate the information that she'd discovered. "Anyway, from what we've been able to uncover about them, they seem to be a bit of a white supremacist group. The star of destiny seems to be their take on the swastika or something similar."

"It kinda fits with Rick's general attitude. Especially if you try talking about politics or anything like that with him!" Mike said, running his mind back to some of the rare conversations that he'd had with the man.

"As far as we can tell, they seem to be attempting to use their negative magic to undermine Western Europe. They want to perpetuate some kind of white power, at least, that's as far as we can tell, at the moment."

"Just a minute, Toni." Mike Dean broke in. "You don't think that Tac's become mixed up with this group as well, do you?"

"I wouldn't have thought so, from what I know of him. To be quite honest, Mike, I think he might have become involved with them, without even realising what's going on." Toni Sillwood suggested. "He could well have become trapped by Rick Fischer's influences. It's possible that he might even have been slipping Tac some subtle drug during the tour. Something to make it easier for him to get into Tac's head."

"Well, at least that might go some way to explaining the mood changes that you've noticed, Mike." Richard Levi said.

"So, you think they've drugged Tac into becoming a part of this Star of Destiny group!" Mike Dean said, he spoke more to himself than to the other two, but they both heard his question.

"Oh, I doubt whether he's actually a part of the group." Richard Levi added, to ease Mike's fears. "If Rick's been drugging him, it's likely to be with something that would reduce his willpower. That would make it easier for them to control his movements, without him realising it. It could be through some kind of simple suggestion or mild hypnosis."

"What I don't understand, is why would they pick on Tac." Mike Dean said, after a few moments. "I mean, he's quite a high profile character, especially in the music world. Wouldn't it make more sense for them to pick on someone less, well, less visible?"

"I'm sure that they would have, if that were possible." Toni Sillwood stated. Opening the folder of documents that she was holding, she pulled out a large sheet of paper. "I drew this up last night, its Tac's birth chart."

"What you mean like a horoscope?" Mike Dean asked.

"No, Mike. This is his birth chart, you can build a horoscope from it, but this is the basic building blocks, if you like."

"Okay Toni, so what's it tell you?"

"Well, one of the things that stands out to me straight away, is the link between the Sun and Mars." Toni Sillwood explained, pointing to some of the symbols in the circle that she'd drawn. "Mars, as you might know, is the god of war. The position of that planet in a chart often goes to show ones' aggressive tendencies. Finding the sun in conjunction to Mars, in the twelfth house and under the sign of Sagittarius doesn't bode well to my way of thinking."

"In what way, Toni? I don't see what you're trying to get at." Mike Dean said.

"Looking at this, I think that they might be trying to use Tac as some kind of figurehead. Let's face it, if it becomes known that he's linked with them, it could be useful to them. His fame might help them in trying to get their message across to more people."

"Okay, Toni, so let's say you're right. Is there anything that we can do to counteract it?"

"To be quite honest, I'm not sure that we can do anything, not at the moment anyway." Toni Sillwood admitted.

"Well… we, we can't sit around here, waiting for something to happen. Tac's off to Germany tomorrow, shouldn't we try to stop him?"

"I agree that we should look at trying to reduce their influence over Tac. The thing is, stopping him from going could alert them to the fact that we're onto them. I'm afraid we've got no choice but to let him go." Richard Levi explained.

"Look, I've got some things I need to tie up, before we can leave for Germany ourselves. I'll leave you to fill Mike in with a bit more detail, if that's okay, Rich." Toni Sillwood said, rising to her feet and heading towards the door. "I'll see you both tomorrow, till then, we've got to be patient and let things go wherever they're going. Now we've got an idea of what's happening, we can work at counteracting it."

As soon as Toni Sillwood left the bookshop, Mike Dean posed the main question that was in his head. Did Richard believe the things that she had told them, he asked, and did he think that they could trust her. In answer, Richard explained how he had managed to track down The Union of the Mountain Ash. They were an organisation that he had only ever heard vague rumours about in the past. It had taken patient probing before he had been able to get to anyone involved with the group. Since speaking to them, he had become convinced that they were genuine. He was happy to throw his weight behind everything that Toni had said.

Taking his old atlas down from the shelf behind him, he opened it once more to the pages that showed Europe. The large orange pentagram inscribed across it, seemed to glow at them. Richard Levi pointed out Hannover, the city that they now knew Tac was heading for. It immediately became clear to them both that it was close to being in the centre of the pentagram. Grabbing another smaller atlas from the table beside him, Richard flicked it open. Leafing through the pages until he came to the ones that covered central Germany in more detail. Pointing to Hannover on the map, he drew Mike's attention to a nearby area marked as the Harz Nature Park. The region was a short distance to the south-east of the city.

He tapped his finger on a spot on the map where two large lakes stood out. Explaining that there were a network of caves laying at the northern end of the lakes that were of interest. Richard explained that Toni believed the area around the caves was where The Star of Destiny would be meeting. Her main reasoning was that the caves had flagged up several times in the past, they had built up a reputation for strange and often dark practices. Among other things, there was a history of witchcraft and devil worship in the area. The cave systems had a long dark history behind them, it was something that made them stand out to Toni. It was the area that they would be looking to head for, once they arrived in Germany.

Over the next hour, Richard Levi explained as much as he could, from everything that Toni Sillwood had told him. The main focus was concentrated on what they were going to achieve in Germany. He explained how Toni was planning to approach the task and what she was hoping they could do. They scoured through the atlases for any possible clues to the area. Looking for anything that could be of interest for their trip. They knew that it was impossible to guess about what they might find in Germany, from looking at the maps. They decided that the more secluded areas, those a little harder to reach, would be the best place to start. Coming to an end of his briefing, Richard said that he would meet Mike at eleven o'clock the next morning.

When he returned home that evening, Mike Dean was happy to find that Wendy had no plans for the night. Suggesting that they went out for dinner, he hoped to break the news to her without causing too much of a drama. He wanted to take time to explain everything to her, so that she would understand. The trip that he was about to make had come out of the blue, especially as he had only recently returned. He was aware that it wouldn't go down too well, as he had only been back from the tour for a few days. When he mentioned his forthcoming trip, Wendy was far from impressed by the news. She listened in taunt silence but once she'd heard what was going on, she expressed her approval. She had known Tac and Sam almost as long as Mike had and didn't want to see any harm come to either of them or Cheyenne. She often looked after Cheyenne, when Sam needed her to and had come to enjoy her time with their busy daughter.

Mike Dean explained that none of them would have a chance to talk to Sam about it all before they left. He asked Wendy if she would be able to fill her in, once they had all left for Germany. He hoped that by the time Sam and Cheyenne flew out to Germany, to meet up with Tac, the whole episode would be over. More to the point, he wanted to find a positive conclusion to the saga. As Sam and Cheyenne were planning on flying out, Mike suggested that Wendy could book some time off. She could travel over with them, and they could all meet up in Hannover. It was a city that he knew well and had always enjoyed. He explained that, he didn't feel that it would be a good idea for Sam and Cheyenne to be flying out on their own. In case anything was to happen, it would be good to have her around as well.

# Thirteen

"Did I tell you about the old man's bedroom?

"Well I managed to pluck up the courage to get in there, to start sorting things out. Had to wade my way through all the rubbish he'd collected over the years.

"Course, I knew that it had to be done, sooner or later, but getting it started seemed too hard to face. It always seems to be the way though, getting my head right to do things. Once I got going, that was it, I would be well away. Found it wasn't actually as bad as I thought it would be.

"Most of what I found there was rubbish, of course. In the bin straight away that lot was; clothes, DVDs, CDs and some of the books I dumped straight away. Obviously, I kept the more interesting books, but there weren't too many of them; a dozen at the most.

"There was a right mix of oddities sitting on the windowsill, when I pulled open the curtain. Half a dozen animal skulls of various sizes, not sure what any of them was but one of them was pretty big.

"Some of the drawers in the two cabinets was a little bit more interesting. There were odd bits and pieces that I thought I might be able to make use of.

"One of those drawers was a real treasure trove!

"All sorts of pointless garbage there. Some half-used candles, a pile of sticks held together by a black ribbon, loads of stuff like that.

"I found a rather neat knife with a curved blade and a carved white handle that I guessed might be ivory. It was sharp too, that blade, cut my finger on it, I did. There was some bits of jewellery with various symbols carved on them. A small silver bowl caught my eye, it looked as if something had been burnt in it. The only other things of interest was a collection of canvas pouches. They contained a right mixture of strange stuff. One of them held a selection of small oval pebbles, they was all completely smooth and shiny.

"Another one of those pouches held a collection of animal bones! They was all shapes and sizes, fuck knows what he was doing with them, but they was all really smooth too. All looked as if they had been well handled.

"Pushed to the back of one of them drawers, concealed by a collection of t-shirts, I found a square black box. It wasn't too big so I almost missed it at first. It was the kind of thing that you might put jewellery in, so I lifted the lid wondering what it might contain. He weren't a jewellery type of man, never known him to wear a wedding ring or anything.

"What I found inside that box was a little strange. There was a plain leather pouch, no more than two inches square at the most and it had the feel of being old, really old. Don't know too much about these things, but I felt it might have been African or American Indian, that kinda thing.

"The leather was solid, stiff and brittle as I lifted the flap up. I wanted to see if it contained anything, what I uncovered was two knots of what I felt sure was human hair!

"One of them bunches was kinda light blonde in colour. The other was dark brown, so dark that it was almost black. Now, why would the old man be holding onto clumps of hair, like that, I asked myself.

"It was yet another one of the old man's mysteries that I'd managed to uncover in the house. Tipping the knots of hair onto the bed, I found that they both appeared to look fresh and new. Didn't look as if they'd been stuffed into an old leather pouch for god knows how long. They had the feeling of having been recently cut, not dry or brittle in any way; I thought that was rather odd.

"Have to admit that looking at those two knots of hair gave me a bit of an idea.

"Could one of them be linked to that bitch witchy woman that was refusing to leave me alone, I wondered. Now if one of them was her hair, well, I could use it to form a doll of some kind. Yeah, could be my own little bit of voodoo.

"Would that help me get her out of my mind? Would I be able to control her that way? I needed something, and wondered whether that would be the way to go.

"I searched through the books and leaflets that I had now collected together in the spare room. I was looking for anything about voodoo dolls but there wasn't much like that. I'd heard about things like that, of course, but didn't know any real details about how to go about it. I remembered reading that you needed something belonging to the person you was trying to influence.

"I didn't know how to go about doing anything like that, but I used my initiative and got on with it. I'm getting quite good at doing things like that.

"I found an old bedsheet stuck in the airing cupboard and ripped it up. Bunching shreds of fabric together and tying them, I set about creating a figure out of the sheet. As I worked at it, I placed the knot of blonde hair at its centre.

"I almost drew a face on it, for effect like, but then I thought that was being a bit stupid, a little bit childish. This weren't no kids' toy I was making, was it?

"Somehow, I had the feeling that if I was right about that hair, it would have to be the blonde hair, not the darker bunch. Fuck knows who that could have come from, or why the old man kept it like that.

"Once I'd created my little poppet, don't know why that name came to my mind but it seemed to fit the figure. Well, then I left it to sit in the spare room, right in the centre of the pentagram. I thought it would be a good way to empower it.

"With that one doll sitting there in the spare room, I turned my thoughts onto how I was going to use it. I needed to get control over the woman, or spirit, or whatever the damned bitch was.

"What I came up with seemed to make some kind of sense, to my mind anyway. You see, I came up with the idea of making a second doll, one with my hair in it, really put myself into it. Then I could use that one to dominate the other one.

"Would it work? Well, I had no idea but it felt like the way to go. I slept with that second doll under my pillow for a night. Hoping that it would pick up on my influence, become a part of me.

"Once I was happy with what I'd done, I brought the two dolls together, with mine engulfing the other one. To keep them together, I bound them up with thick lengths of that sheet material.

"Later that night, I brought out my mirror once again. I wanted to see if I could still see her and, more importantly, whether there had been any changes. See if anything had happened.

"Well, I was in for a bit of a surprise, wasn't I?

"Yeah, she was still there, glaring at me aggressively. I tried not to laugh when I saw her, she seemed to have cloth wrapped all around the lower part of her face. She looked almost like a damned Egyptian mummy. I could see that she was fighting against it, she seemed to know that it was me that'd done it to her. I could tell that from her eyes. Oh, yes, she knew it was me alright."

# Fourteen

After getting up early to prepare for the forthcoming trip, Mike Dean tried to relax. He had a quiet breakfast with Wendy then carried his bag out to the car. Shortly before eleven o'clock, he drove down the busy street and pulled up in front of Levi's Books, running the car up onto the curb to allow the steady stream of traffic to pass him. He didn't want to leave the car, so pressed the horn to tell Richard Levi that he was there. Seeing Jamie looking out of the window to see what was going on, he waved to signal his arrival. Richard stepped out of the shop five minutes later, which was perfect timing. A few moments earlier, Mike had caught sight of a traffic warden heading down the street in his direction. Opening the rear door, Richard dropped his bag onto the back seat before sliding into the passenger seat.

Richard Levi's directions led Mike through a maze of back streets, until he had lost any point of reference. A short time later, he found himself driving down through the centre of Fulham. They were heading towards Toni Sillwood's large semi-detached house in Wyatt Drive. Richard had told him that it was close to Bishops Park but that meant nothing to Mike, so he had to rely on the directions. The two bags that Mike and Richard had brought with them sat squashed into the corner of the boot. A large flight case, that Toni said she needed to take with her alongside her backpack, filled the rest of the space. When she had first come out to the car, Toni had refused to have the case put into the boot. She stated that it was far too valuable for her to let out of her sight.

After a time of awkward twisting and turning it became clear that the case wouldn't fit on the back seat, not if Toni Sillwood was going to fit in the car as well. In the end, she agreed to have the case stashed away behind her, as long as they locked the boot. On the drive through to Heathrow Airport, Toni found herself fielding a barrage of questions. They asked about what was in her case that was so valuable and why she was taking it to Germany with her. No matter how hard they pressed, all she was willing to tell them was that it contained a powerful talisman. It was one that could only be used in the most extreme of circumstances.

To change the subject from the contents of her case, Toni Sillwood told them about the meeting that had taken place the previous evening. She had met up with some members from the inner circle of The Union of the Mountain Ash. It was rare for someone who wasn't a part of the inner circle to be allowed into a gathering of that kind. The union members had been debating how to approach the whole situation late into the night. They had been trying to agree on a plan of action, something that Toni could work from. One of the main subjects that had come up was whether she should have access to the talisman. It was something that a couple of the members had suggested, believing that it might be of use. Although Toni had no direct entry to the highest level of meetings, her contact kept her informed about what was going on. In the early hours of the morning, they managed to reach an uneasy agreement. They allowed her to take the talisman to Germany with her, but under a strict set of rules.

The talisman was a powerful symbol to the union, under normal circumstances it rarely left the vaults beneath the union's headquarters. It would usually only come out once or twice a year, often to coincide with solstice ceremonies. They had entrusted Toni with the talisman but a few of the inner circle were still unhappy with the idea. The thought of it leaving the country had caused much debate, especially amongst some of the more staunch minded members. The main warning was that its power was far too great to entrust to someone outside the inner circle. The final vote, when it came in the early hours of the morning, had been a narrow one. Toni's contact wouldn't tell her exactly how close the decision had been, but said that there was a fine margin. The fact that they gave Toni access to the talisman, showed how worried they were by the ongoing events.

The trios arrival at Heathrow Airport, finally put a stop to the flood of questions about the talisman. Toni Sillwood would say nothing more but as a final point she told them that they shouldn't mention it in public. The first problem that they hit, as they made their way through the airport security, came due to Toni's case. She insisted that it had to stay with her as hand baggage; she would not hear of it going into the hold with the other luggage. When they reached the security gate, Toni refused to open the case for any reason and the staff manning the scanners found the case impossible to penetrate. It all added suspicion about what might be hiding inside.

A few moments of intense debate with the security guard who had stopped them ensued. In the end Toni Sillwood pulled a sheath of official looking documents from her pocket. Trying not to create a scene, she handed them to the head of security. He had joined his colleague to find out what was going on, noticing the hold up at the scanners. Something in the man's expression changed the moment that he glanced down at the top paper. It was clear that he was impressed by the paperwork, as he looked over the cover page. Mike and Richard passed through the gates to the departure lounge without any trouble and waited to find out what would happen. Seeing them standing there, Toni waved them off, saying that she would join them soon. An official in a bland, colourless suit led Toni off in a different direction altogether. It was more than twenty minutes later when Toni reappeared, still clutching her precious case. They were now ready to board the plane.

Once they had taken their seats on the plane, Toni Sillwood explained what had happened. The Union had foreseen the problems of carrying the case through customs, and they had tried their best to help. With that in mind, Toni had come prepared with some special paperwork, to use if she hit a problem. The documentation had been arranged by a member of the inner circle of the union. She was a high level government minister and was happy to draw up the warrants to sanction their flight. The papers allowed Toni to proceed through with little problem. She had been hoping that there would have been no reason to use them. It was something that could draw attention to them and arouse unwanted interest in what they were up to.

If the Star of Destiny found the talisman was heading in their direction, it could have a massive effect on their arrangements. It was something that could be more than enough to force the group into changing their plans. The talisman was a well known phenomenon in many circles, although more by rumour than any actual contact. Part of the agreement to let the talisman leave the vaults was that as few people as possible found out about it. They also stated that Toni should only use it in extreme circumstances, if there was no other way. One of the members of the inner circle was a high up government official and had been able to draw up the paperwork. If she needed to use it, they knew it would ease her journey through any security issues.

Once they reached their seats on the plane, the flight to Germany continued without a problem. The trip proved to be calm and relaxing when they finally took off. Arriving in Hannover, they found that everything went far smoother than on their departure. The official that Toni had dealt with at Heathrow had contacted his German counterparts. Advising them of the groups imminent arrival, he managed to clear the way through security for them. Leaving the plane, the party found themselves having almost VIP treatment. The way through the terminal and out of the airport was completed easily. Heading towards the exit, Tony expressed her concern about their treatment. She was worried that it could be something that might draw attention to their arrival.

A taxi was waiting for them and within half an hour of setting down in Germany, they were on the way to the hotel. Richard Levi had booked them into it for the first night, so they could get their bearings. It was early in the evening by the time that they settled into their small but comfortable rooms. The travel chaos was now well behind them. The whole thing, since the previous evenings meeting, had been a mad rush to Mike Dean's mind. In contrast, from the moment that they had boarded the plane, he had noticed a subtle shift in the pace of everything. The sense of urgency that had been hanging around them and the previous pressure had evaporated away. Now that they had arrived in Germany, a sense of calm had settled over them. Mike was uncomfortable with the situation, after all the pressure to get to Germany.

Mike Dean was aware that they still had some way to travel, before they reached their destination. His uneasy feeling came because now they were in Hannover, all the urgency had dissipated. There was no great rush for them to travel any further towards their ultimate goal. Toni Sillwood was talking about spending the night relaxing in a local restaurant. Now the immediate pressure of reaching Germany was over, they could ease off. Mike found the change in mood strange and a little hard to accept, after all the previous pressure that they had been under and the hastily arrange flights. It was the first question that Mike wanted to ask, once the three of them met up in the hotel bar, later that evening.

"Well, I told you that I had a meeting with members of the inner circle, last night." Toni Sillwood said, when Mike Dean asked about the change in pace. "Well, we had a good look at all the information that we were able to gather, last night. We're now confident that we have a few days leeway, a little bit of time to play with."

"So, why the mad rush to get over here then, Toni?"

"Oh, I think it's far better for us to be somewhere in the area, in case something unexpected were to happen. If something were to go down and we were still back in London, we'd be stuck. There wouldn't have been anything that we could have done about it, would there?"

"Okay, I guess I can see that, Toni. So, what else did you manage to find out about all this, is there anything that you haven't told us yet?" Mike Dean questioned, sure that something wasn't being said. He couldn't help feeling that some vital piece of information was being withheld from him.

"Ah, well… there's a new moon on Friday night. Being in the sign of Leo, the inner circle believe that things are leading us towards that date. It would make a certain amount of sense."

"You don't sound too convinced!"

"Yeah, well, it's hard to be sure about any of these things, without knowing exactly what they've got planned." Toni

Sillwood explained, adding. "All I can say is that there is a certain logic behind the idea. It wouldn't be surprising if things happened, or at least starting to happen on that date."

"So, what do we do now? What's our next move going to be?"

"Mike, for now, we need to sit tight, have a good meal and as far as possible, a relaxing evening. Then we will all be far better prepared to make our next move, tomorrow."

"So, what will be our next move, Toni?" Richard Levi asked, having been rather quiet since they had met up in the bar.

"Well, the first thing we need to do tomorrow, is to check out the general area that we're targeting. See if we can find any signs that something might be about to go down."

"Meanwhile we sit here and hope that Tac's alright." Mike Dean said in an undertone, almost too quietly for the other two to hear.

"Mike, I do understand how you feel, really I do." Toni Sillwood said, having caught his comment. "But there's nothing that we can do tonight. The site we're heading for is almost a hundred kilometres away and only the first half of that is motorway. From there it's all lesser roads, it's going to take a while."

"Yeah, I realise that, Toni. It's just that I'm finding it a bit frustrating, not being able to do anything."

"Oh, don't worry, Mike. I've got a feeling that there's going to be plenty for us to do, once this all starts to flow."

"Yeah, I guess you're right, Toni. Just a bit impatient, I would prefer to be doing something."

"Anyway, I've arranged for a hire car to arrive for us, it's due to arrive first thing tomorrow morning. So it would be pointless trying to rush off into the night at this point." Toni Sillwood explained, finally putting the matter to bed.

"Yeah, okay." Mike Dean said, shaking his head, knowing that he had been beaten. "It's just, after all the rush to get over here, sitting around like this doesn't seem quite right."

"Don't worry, things will spark up soon enough, Mike." Richard Levi said.

The rest of the evening crept passed but it was pleasant enough for the three of them. Richard Levi finding himself acting as a bit of a buffer between the other two. Mike Dean wanted to be doing something, at least drawing up a plan of attack, something for them to work to. Toni Sillwood, was not willing to rush in, wanting to discover what they were facing first. Richard had an idea of how stressful the following few days could turn out to be for them. He emphasised the point that if they rested and were in top condition, they'd be able to cope with everything that was to come far better. There would be plenty of time to discuss their plan of attack on the drive through to the Harz National Park. If Toni was right that nothing was going to happen until the Friday, at the earliest, then they had plenty of time.

# Fifteen

The wait in the hotel's reception area for the hire car that Toni Sillwood had booked dragged on for hours. When it finally arrived, it was a little after ten o'clock. That was over an hour later than the nine o'clock booking, the driver having driven to the wrong hotel at first. From there he managed to get lost trying to find them, even though Toni had confirmed the address with him. Shortly after eleven they were in the car and on the A7 Autobahn heading southward. Mike Dean was happy to volunteer to take the first driving stint. He was dying to get on with things and didn't want to be sitting in the passenger seat, watching the countryside roll by. At least if he was behind the wheel, he knew that he would feel as if he was doing something.

Once they were cruising down the Autobahn, Toni Sillwood ran though her proposed plan of action. She talked about various targeted areas that she was looking for them to head to. They were places that she had decided they should investigate in the days ahead. The main aim for that first day was to reach the town of Herzberg on the Sieber River. It was a town that stood on the southwestern side of the nature park. Toni had planned for them to set up their home base there, a safe haven that they could operate from. From that town, it would only take a short drive to reach the regions that they were targeting. The area that surrounded the lakes would be their main focus of attention. Toni didn't want to stay any closer to the lakes, in case their presence caught anyone's attention. She was well aware that, as strangers to the area, they were likely to stand out.

The main reason that Toni Sillwood was attracted to Herzberg was that it was close to another cave system. It was one that she was hoping would be similar to what they would find when they reached their final destination. She wanted a chance to look round those caves, in case they were unable to get anywhere near to the area they were targeting. Toni was sure that any scraps of information that they could pick up might help them in the long run.

If everything went to plan, Toni was hoping to make an initial trip up to the lakes, the following day. She was sure that travelling up to the caves during the day wouldn't be too much of a problem. Toni knew that she was being a little over cautious, in case they couldn't get there for any reason. If they were close to the Herzberg caves, it would prove to be a backup plan. Toni expected to find that the caves and the area around them would be busy with sightseers during the day. That way they would be able to become lost in the crowds as they checked out the lay of the land.

The next morning, they were up early having had a restful night. They were now eager to start investigating, all wanting to get on with the day. After a quick breakfast consisting of coffee and little else, they made their way out to the car. To start with, they were planning on heading towards the nearby village of Elbingerode. Several old mining sites were near to the village, including a large open-cast limestone mine. They found a spot where they could park on the outskirts of the town, with little trouble, everything seemingly quiet and peaceful. Leaving the car behind, they walked through the picturesque landscape, heading in the direction of the river Bode.

Reaching the cave system, they could make out one of the lakes through the dense treeline. The still waters sat in the distance, at the bottom of the valley. Everything looked peaceful and idyllic to their eyes. There was no sign of anything untoward, no groups of strange people hanging around, other than them. In fact, it was all far too serene, to Mike Dean's mind. Although he didn't voice that opinion to the other two, not wanting to spook them. As they strolled around, they met several groups of people out enjoying the warm sunshine. They encountered a group of school kids scurrying around one of the cave entrances. The children were making a lot of noise as they ran about. There was nothing at all to hint at anything unusual going on, as far as they could see. Despite that, Toni Sillwood said that she was now certain that they had come to the right area.

The whole thing came down to a matter of energy, Toni Sillwood explained. She could sense it flowing through the site, feeling like a mild static charge to her. Whether it was as simple as the convergence of ley lines or something else completely, she wasn't sure. Whatever happened it was there, an unmistakable impression that altered the atmosphere of the area. An hour later, they found themselves surrounded by another group of school kids. The second party were older and more boisterous than the previous crowd. Toni decided that it was the ideal time for them to leave the area. There was nothing else that they could do at that time.

It was unlikely that anything would happen during the day, Toni Sillwood explained. Now that they had an idea of how the site looked, she decided that it was better for them to leave. She didn't want their presence to become noticed and possibly arouse suspicion. Especially if someone was on the lookout for people acting in an unusual way. It would now be far better for them to leave the area. The last thing that she wanted them to do was draw attention to their presence, if anyone from the Star of Destiny group was on the site. She was aware that hanging around without reason could draw attention to them.

With that in mind, Richard Levi pointed out the town of Quedlinburg, which was a short drive away. Studying the map that he'd brought with him, he showed them that there was a castle marked, standing near to the town. They all decided that a little bit of sightseeing would be the ideal, low-key, way for them to spend the rest of the afternoon. They would become tourists for a couple of hours and hopefully blend into the background. With luck, it would also take their minds of everything for a while. The castle proved to be a good example of medieval architecture and the surrounding grounds managed to hold the party's attention for a couple of hours.

Late in the afternoon, having been on their feet for some time, they walked through into the town. They were hoping to find a restaurant, somewhere they could sit down and eat. In the late afternoon sunlight, they strolled through the quaint streets, taking in the view. The timber framed houses of the old town looked impressive, caught in the sun. The architecture showed them how old the town was, with its long history dating back to the ninth century. Toni Sillwood was planning for them to return to the caves again later that evening. They would have to travel in that direction on the way back to the hotel, so they wouldn't be going out of their way. It appeared to be the ideal scenario; they could stop off on the way back.

By nine o'clock that evening, they had eaten a good meal and had a couple of light drinks. Then Toni Sillwood decided that she was ready for them to make their next move. By that time even Richard Levi had been showing the first signs of restlessness. He had become slightly agitated, unable to sit still for long. Although it was still light, the summer night not having taken over yet, the road was quiet and empty of traffic. They drove through the tree covered hills and parked up in a secluded area off the main road. They had a little bit of a hike to reach their destination, but they were looking forward to the walk. Toni was wary that driving any nearer to the site could draw unwanted attention to them.

Taking a thin trail that led through the valley they headed south, at times fighting with dense clumps of undergrowth, they made their way to the river. From there, they planned to follow the track until they were close to the caves themselves. It was an indirect route, but there would be less chance of bumping into anyone by going that way. There was the possibility that someone might be hanging around, looking out for strangers.

Mike Dean was thinking that they had completely missed their mark. It appeared as if they were lost in the maze of undergrowth, now that they were in the deepening twilight. He was about to mention it when Toni Sillwood hushed them. Indicating that she had spotted something ahead of them, she stopped them in their tracks. Motioning for them to duck down, like some military leader in the field, she crept forward. Taking to her hands and knees, she crawled through the dense brush covering the area. Mike and Richard followed, trying hard not to make a sound. Toni was far more athletic and able to cope with the terrain than the other two. Crawling along on hands and knees, they managed to keep up with her, somehow.

After a couple of minutes, they found a spot where they could see through the packed treeline. In front of them, they could make out several points of flickering light glowing in the descending twilight. Creeping a little closer, they made for a spot where they could get a reasonable view of what was going on. Six large flaming torches stood in front of a cave, casting a flickering light over the flat area. They could see around thirty people milling about in an aimless display of restlessness. The crowd were chatting amongst themselves as if they were at a social event, but it was clear they were waiting for something to happen.

As far as they could see, a large part of the crowd consisted of spiky haired punks and skinheads. Sprinkled amongst them were a few people who defied description. The rest of the assembly had an intense look, many with severe, sour expressions on their faces. The one thing that stood out were the armbands that everyone in the crowd was wearing. They were black with large white circles containing a symbol that looked like interlocking triangles. Although Mike Dean couldn't place the symbol, he was certain that he had come across it before somewhere. He thought that it could have been amongst the books that he had seen Richard going through back at his shop.

Crouching in the undergrowth, they watched the crowd drift around with little purpose. After a time they noticed a definite change of attitude in the gathering. At first it affected those close to the cave but soon the new attitude swept over everyone in the clearing. One by one, they all turned their attention towards the entrance. Within a short space of time the whole area had become engulfed in silence. The crowd appeared to be rooted to the spot, as four figures stepped out from the shadows of the cave. As they entered into the torchlight the assembled gathering, as one, gave a clenched fist salute. It was only when the two men leading the group moved to one side, that Mike Dean spotted Tac at the back of the gang. He appeared to be paying little attention to what was going on around him, as far as Mike could tell. His eyes firmly fixed onto a spot on the ground, a few feet ahead of him.

The session that followed continued for a little over half an hour. During that time, two speakers extolled the massed assembly into taking some kind of action. Throughout the meeting, the only interruptions came from odd shouts and cheers. Other than that, the crowd stood in awed reverence. From where Mike viewed the scene, it was impossible for him to make out what was actually being said. Going by the crowd's demeanour, they seemed to be appreciating every word of it.

Forty minutes passed, then the speakers gave the clenched fist salute to the crowd. Mike Dean looked on, trying to work out what might happen next. The salute was echoed by the rest of the onlookers, signalling that the meeting had now come to a close. The two main speakers walked away from the clearing and stepped back into the cave. Tac and another man trailing along behind them. From where Mike Dean had been watching, it had been impossible to make out what had been going on in any detail. He had been sitting amid a tangle of brambles, narrowly avoiding a growth of stinging nettles. He couldn't help feeling that what they had seen was little more than a political rally. One with rather right-wing overtones, he realised, but still a political rally of some kind.

Other than the strange symbol on the armbands and the salutes, it had all appeared to be rather innocuous. As far as Mike could tell, the added extras were more for effect than anything. Not for the first time since his arrival in Germany, he was beginning to wonder what he was doing there. There seemed to be little of the dark things that Toni had been talking about going on. The one concern that he did have though, was the expression that he had been able to make out on Tac's face. His body language was all wrong and that expression was almost completely blank. From a distance, It looked as if he couldn't take in what was happening around him. Now that the meeting had run its course, the crowd began to disperse. Some headed into the surrounding area, others making their way straight up the main trail.

It didn't take long before Mike heard various vehicles starting up in the distance, followed by the sounds of cars fading into the night. Soon enough the whole area was shrouded in silence once again, as the night settled in around the region. Mike was about to get to his feet, his legs feeling stiff and awkward from crouching down for so long. At that moment, Toni Sillwood put her hand on his arm, warning him not to make another move. As he froze in place, the four men that he had forgotten about, strolled out of the cave. They wasted no time in making their way up the hill, still with Tac walking along amongst them.

Once they had given the group plenty of time to clear the area, Toni Sillwood finally rose to her feet and stretched. Her movement signalled that the coast now appeared to be deserted. As soon as possible they followed the trail back towards the river. It was a trek that was far harder now that the full darkness of the night had descended on them. The torches that they had with them seemed ineffective against the dense trees. Shadows engulfed them as they walked through the woodland, their footing unsteady on the uneven ground. In the end, they managed to make their way back to where they had parked the car.

It was one o'clock in the morning by the time that they reached the quiet hotel in Herzberg. Arriving at that hour of the night took the desk clerk by surprise. He didn't appear to like having guests turn up at that time of the day and was a little flustered at first. Once he realised that they were booked in, everything calmed down, and he allowed them to go up to their rooms. They were all feeling tired after the day's events and made the way to the lifts without another word. Despite his fatigue, Mike Dean found it impossible to sleep that night. Twisting and turning, he tried in vain to make himself comfortable. Visions of Tac's blank, listless expression overpowering his mind.

# Sixteen

The next morning Mike Dean woke from his troubled night's sleep feeling tired and a little confused. His head was full of questions that he couldn't work out the answers to. Meeting Toni Sillwood for a late breakfast, he tried to put some of his questions to her straight away. Toni insisted that it would be better to wait for Richard Levi to join them before she went over things. When they were all together, she would say more about everything that they had seen the previous evening. Half an hour later, Richard finally joined them in the hotel lounge. Before doing anything, they ordered another tray of coffee and pastries. As soon as the waitress had walked away from their table, Mike jumped straight in with his first point. His impatience having been growing in intensity as he waited.

"Look, Toni, you've told us about these magical influences that you believe in."

"Believe me, Mike, they're out there. They're all around us."

"Yeah? Well, you've told us what you think the inscriptions that I saw on those bricks mean and everything else. All I saw last night was a bunch of, what looked to me like, neo-Nazi's having some kind of moonlight political rally! I don't see how all this, this magic of yours fits in with what we saw."

"Oh, I'm pretty sure there was a lot more to last night than a political rally, Mike. Let's face it, we couldn't actually hear what was being said from where we were, could we?"

"Come on, Toni, you're reading all sorts of things into what was little more than a political gathering. One that Tac has somehow become involved in. Although god knows why he's become involved, it doesn't seem to make any sense!"

"Mike, I can understand your feelings about all this and, yes, I agree with you, it is frustrating. Still, I think we should let Toni guide us on this." Richard Levi said, as he drained his coffee cup and refilled it.

"I'm trying to, Rich, believe me, I am, but it's just... oh, I don't know..."

"Come on, Toni. Surely you can tell us something more. Give us something to work with. We need to know what we're getting ourselves into." Richard said.

"Well, I'll try to put it into basic terms. The best way that I can describe this whole thing is the nurturing of negative energy." Toni Sillwood said. Before speaking she glanced around the lounge, to see if anyone was paying any attention to them. They could tell that she wanted to make sure that no one was close enough to hear what she was saying. "There are powerful energy sources everywhere, they're all around us. At the confluences of ley lines they can be very strong, like the ones we found up at the caves. If they're tapped into, they can be used in many ways, for good or for bad."

"Sure, I can see that, you told us about that before, but how does it work here?"

"Mike, violence is a major source of negative energy. It can be used a bit like a giant sponge to suck up positive energy. I'm sure that's the kind of thing that we're dealing with here. For some reason this group are trying to focus a negative field of energy, so that they can use it for some purpose. I must admit that its real purpose is something that I can't work out at the moment, though."

"That symbol we all saw on the armbands they were all wearing, Toni. Does that symbol mean anything to you, I can't help feeling that I've seen it before, somewhere. It looked to me something like several interlocking triangles."

"Yeah, I noticed them too, Mike. I had to look it up on the web this morning, to be sure. As far as I can tell that symbol is one called a Valknut, it comes from Norse mythology. As far as I can see, it seems to represent the power over life and death. That's not particularly political but they seem to be using the symbol as some kind of a rallying point."

With the day now passing them by and the second coffee pot having disappeared, they needed a new plan. Agreeing that nothing was likely to happen until the evening, at the earliest, they now had the afternoon to fill. Toni Sillwood mentioned that the town of Goslar was a short drive away. She had found a selection of town guides in the hotel's reception and picked that one out of the pile. Goslar sounded like a busy place. It had a regular weekly market and was the site of several museums, one that was located in the gothic town hall. Another point of interest was a theatre that had made its home in an old disused power station.

As it was a warm sunny day, Toni Sillwood suggested that they could drive up and spend the afternoon in Goslar. Mike Dean was more than happy to go on the trip, he was hoping that it would take his mind off of things for a little while. Richard decided to stay in Herzberg, wanting to have a quiet afternoon. He said that he needed to rest up so that he was ready for whatever might happen next. Agreeing to meet up again that evening, Mike and Toni set out on the trip northwards towards Goslar. It wasn't long before they passed a sign saying they were two kilometres away from the town. At that moment a car appeared in the rear-view mirrors. As they continued, the dark blue Mercedes overtook them, travelling a little too fast for the road.

When it was level with them, Mike glanced over, wary of its passing speed. He was driving at the time and had noticed the Mercedes appearing in the distance, heading towards them fast. He couldn't help wondering why it was in such a rush. As the car flashed by them, he glanced across questioning once again why it was in such a hurry. Straight away he recognised the figure who was sitting in the back seat of the car, staring out of the window.

"Hey, Toni! That was Tac in the back of that Merc!" He shouted, pointing at the departing tail-lights. The car took a tight bend in the road and disappeared into the distance.

"Are you sure?" Toni Sillwood asked. She had been looking at the countryside on the other side of the road and hadn't taken any notice of the car as it passed them.

"Yeah, definitely. I'd know him anywhere." Mike Dean replied, putting his foot down on the accelerator. He was going to try to catch up with the retreating Mercedes.

"Try not to get too close." Toni Sillwood warned. They spotted the Mercedes, once again, as it disappeared around another tight bend in the road. "We don't want them to spot us. Did you notice how many people there were in the car?"

"Just Tac and the driver." Mike Dean said, although he wasn't entirely sure about that fact, the car having passed them in a flash.

After accelerating for a few minutes they soon came within sight of the Mercedes again. It appeared to have eased down on its speed a little, as they drew nearer to the town and the traffic started to get heavier. With the extra cars on the road, Mike Dean found that he could get a little bit closer to the Mercedes. He was now able to leaving a couple of cars between them and still have a reasonable view of it. Driving into the centre of the town, they watched the Mercedes park up near to the railway station.

Mike Dean found a space a few hundred yards further up the road. Pulling into the gap between two other cars, he shut off the engine. Toni Sillwood and Mike sat there looking out of the side window. They were able to see Tac and the driver as they climbed out of the car and stood there for a few moments. After a short discussion, the driver walked up the road towards where Mike had parked. Passing them by, without a second glance in their direction, he marched away in a determined fashion. It was as the man drew closer that they recognised him, he was the man who had been standing next to Tac at the previous night's meeting.

The man walked off up the street and disappeared around a corner, heading away from the town centre. Tac had now been left standing there in the street on his own, beside the locked car. He looked across at the nearby buildings, for a moment he seemed lost and unsure of what he should do next. In time, he appeared to come to a decision and walked off in the direction of the station. Scrambling out of the car, Mike checked that there was no sign of the driver, before setting off in Tac's footsteps. Toni saying that she didn't want to chance him jumping onto a train and disappearing. For a moment they lost sight of him in the milling crowds hanging around the station area. A second later, Toni spotted him walking into a coffee shop and grabbed Mike's arm to point him out.

"Mike, you know him far better than I do." Toni Sillwood said, as they sat down at a table outside the same shop. She ordered some drinks from a loitering, bored looking waiter, before adding. "Go in and see if you can get him talking, let's see if we can draw him away somehow. Don't try to force things though. We don't want to cause any problems and don't forget, he might be here to meet some of that group from last night. I'm rather surprised they've left him here, on his own, it all seems rather odd."

"Yeah, okay Toni, I'll see if I can get anything out of him."

"I'll stay out here, that way I can keep an eye open for that driver, in case he returns."

"What do you think I should tell him?" Mike Dean asked, as he rose to his feet.

"Try not to tell him anything in detail, keep everything as vague as possible. Try to make it seem like the most natural thing in the world to meet him here, act as if you're back home, meeting him in a local pub." Toni Sillwood said, adding. "See if you can draw him away from here, in case someone's coming to meet him. With luck we can get him to come back to the hotel with us, get him out of the area completely. From what I've seen so far, I'm pretty sure that he must be in some kind of mild trance-like state. If that's the case, it'll take some time to break it. If I'm right about that, then we can't just leap in as that could cause unexpected problems."

With all that Toni Sillwood had said rolling around in the back of his head, Mike Dean walked into the coffee shop. Looking at the surrounding tables, he made his way to the back of the half empty room. Noticing a sign pointing to the toilets, he turned towards them. As he couldn't see him, he decided that Tac might have gone off in that direction. He was part of the way through the haphazardly placed tables, when he spotted Tac. He was sitting alone at a secluded table in one shadowy corner, staring into the depths of a cup of hot chocolate.

"Hi Tac, how's it going?" Mike Dean asked, walking over and trying to keep a bright friendly tone to his voice. Without another word, he slipped into the seat opposite his old friend.

"Hello Mike, I…" Tac started to say something more but seemed a little confused and stumbled over his words. "It… it's good to see you. What, what are you doing here?" He asked distractedly, a vacant expression crossing his face.

Now that he was close up to Tac, Mike Dean could see how dishevelled he was looking. He was in distinct need of a shave, which was very unusual for him. He had something against stubble and had always tried to avoid it as much as possible. From what Mike could see, it looked as if he'd been sleeping in the clothes that he was wearing. His shirt and jeans were crumpled and much the worse for wear, like Tac himself.

"Oh, I'm just taking some time out, getting away from things for a bit." Mike Dean replied. He was trying to use phrases that he could remember Tac having said in his note to Sam, before asking. "Are you okay, Tac?"

"Yeah, I… I'm okay. Just, just a bit tired. I… I need some time to myself, time to think."

"What've you got planned now?" Mike Dean asked. "Fancy a drink? I was about to meet up with Toni Sillwood, you remember Toni, from the agency?"

"Yeah…" Tac said, uncertainly. "Yeah, I remember her." There was an emptiness to his voice, little sign of any emotion in it. It almost felt to Mike as if he didn't believe a word of what he was saying. "I guess a quick drink would be good." He added without much conviction.

Walking out of the coffee shop with Tac in tow, Mike Dean

tried to keep up a largely one-sided conversation. Looking around the area, he noticed a small bar a few hundred yards further down the road. There were a collection of tables in front of it, spilling out across the pedestrianised area. Making sure that Toni Sillwood had spotted them, he signalled for her to follow. The bar was quiet when they reached it, with only three people perched at the bar, involved in a noisy game of cards. A young couple sitting at one of the outdoor tables, staring into each other's eyes, were the only customers outside.

Mike walked straight inside, wanting to be out of sight of anyone that might be passing. Picking out a table close to the door but away from the main window, he sat down and glanced again at Tac. A few moments later, Toni Sillwood strolled in and joined them. The lone barman finally managed to drag himself away from the computer screen that he was intent on. Taking their order, he returned a few minutes later with the drinks. Once the barman had retreated back to the bar and his computer screen, Toni began talking to Tac. She asked him about everything that he had been doing over the past few days and who the driver of the car had been.

It soon became clear that Tac couldn't tell them too much about what had been going on. He explained that he had been staying near the station, but he couldn't give them a street name or any other details. The driver was called Hendrik, Tac said, but that was all he knew about the man. He was someone who turned up to drive him around every now and then. When Toni Sillwood asked him what his plans were for the rest of the day, Tac said that he had nothing to do. He wasn't expecting to see Hendrik again for at least a couple of days. That was exactly the kind of thing what Toni wanted to hear. Within minutes, she had convinced Tac to return to the hotel with them.

Leaving half-finished drinks behind them, they quickly made their way back to the car. Trying to act as natural as possible, they continued watching out for anyone who might be looking for Tac. Walking up the road, they noticed that the blue Mercedes had now disappeared, a battered Volkswagen having taken the parking space. There were still plenty of people milling around the station, and Mike hoped that would make them harder to see. As far as they could tell, no one was paying any attention to them. Mike Dean drove away with a sharp intake of breath. He had been sure that someone would jump out of the crowd to try to stop them from driving away.

No one had paid any attention to them, it appeared that no one had been placed there to keep an eye on Tac. As far as they could tell, he had been left to his own devices, which seemed odd to Mike. Once again, he couldn't shake off the feeling of unease that flooded over him. It was all far too simple, far too easy. Their meeting up with Tac like they had, him agreeing to come off with them, it all felt wrong. The idea that no one had been there to stop them, it didn't make any sense. Tac sat in the passenger seat, staring at the passing countryside in silence. As far as they could tell, he was completely disinterested in the whole journey. Mike tried to chat as they set off, making undemanding comments about the situation. It soon became clear that he was wasting his time, so he gave up and studied his friend's behaviour instead.

Reaching the hotel, Tac asked for directions to the bathroom. He explained that drinking early in the day, always went straight through him. Mike Dean took that chance to ask Toni Sillwood her opinion on the situation, admitting that he was concerned about Tac's general demeanour. It was obvious that he wasn't feeling himself, there was a distracted aura hanging over him. To

Mike, it looked as if Tac was sleepwalking through the day, largely unaware of what was going on around him. Toni said that she was now certain that Tac was under the control of some outside influence.

Tac seemed to be in an almost trance-like state. Toni Sillwood was well aware that they would have to tread with care, if they wanted to pull him out of it without causing a problem. She was cautious of the mental damage that she could cause by jumping in too soon, while trying to snap Tac out of it. The most important thing was creating a more stable atmosphere for him. They needed somewhere that they could keep an eye on him and work to remove whatever bonds were holding him. Now that he was at the hotel with them, it should be easy for Toni to look for some chink or loophole that might appear. She would search for a way to break the mental barriers that were inhibiting him.

# Seventeen

"Well, I've got them all now, got them buggers just where I want them! They're totally under my control now. They'll do exactly what I want them to.

"They make a great smokescreen they do, the bloody Star of Destiny!

"And the best thing about it all; I've got them to believe that it's all their own idea. They think they came to me, asking for my help! That's good that is, that's really good.

"I've managed to warp all their white power crap; I've twisted it around on them. Now they think I'm someone who's here to help them along, help them to get what they want.

"You try asking them what's going on, ask them what it is they want. You'll be surprised; they won't be able to find an answer to that question.

"See, I've corrupted their minds, I've got in there, and they don't realise it. Mindless scum, the lot of them, not got a brain cell between them, but they'll follow my suggestions all the way. They'll do exactly what I want them to do.

"I've been working on them rituals over the past few weeks. Moulding them, refining the details, finalising exactly what I need to do for them to work my way. I can pretty much build my own rituals now, no need to search the books for what I want anymore.

"I just let them come to me. I feel like some great radio receiver, picking up the signals from the airwaves. Course, I don't know where they're coming from but I'm picking them up fine, so why should I care where they've come from.

"Course, I don't want to rush any of this, that way I could easily make a mistake. I can take my time with it, there's no great hurry. Just want to make sure that I gets it right, I'm pretty sure I'll only have one chance at getting this right.

"Got that Tac geezer under my control too. I needed to make sure of that, specially once I looked into his daughter's star charts. Her birth line is perfect for me, she'll be that little added extra that will take everything to the next level.

"Oh, that will be great, that will! Using the blood of the daughter, taken by the father! Oh yeah, that will add so much to the ritual, make it far more powerful.

"These entities like their blood, they do, and it doesn't have to be very much. A few drops can work wonders but more than a few, well, who knows where that could take me.

"Thought I'd have to use some of my own blood at first, or one of my bods, but that was before I discovered her. Don't know what made me look into her charts, it just came to me out of nowhere, but I'm really fucking glad that I did.

"Yeah, I'm all powerful now, I am!

"It won't be long before I'll have the world at my feet. Soon everyone will know my name, know what I stand for. When I have Baphomet beside me, I will be in control.

"Those scumbag politicians, think they can tell us all what to do. Those people who tried to fuck me over, they'll all pay. They don't know who I am, don't know what I'm capable of. Soon, soon they will, soon they'll know and then I'll have them cowering before me.

"Course, they'll all want to know me then, won't they? Yeah, course they will.

"They'll all want to be my friend, want to save themselves but I know them. I know what they did, what they thought of me, and they'll pay for it, I'll make sure they pay.

"There's one slight worry that I've got though, one little hiccup that my radar has picked up. I've recently heard that Mike Dean, Tac's mate, and that Toni woman from the Union are over here. Don't know what they've come to Germany for but the timing seems to be a little bit suspicious to me. Are they on to me? Don't see how they can be, I'm sure I've been far too careful but you never know, have I slipped up somewhere?

"One of the blokes from the Star works at the airport. He heard about them as there was some issue over one of their bags or something. Whatever happened, they got rushed through the arrivals lounge like bloody VIP's. Could be a bit of a problem that, still, if I find out they're meddling in my affairs, I could always set the Star of Destiny on them. A little riot outside their hotel, a little explosion inside; anything could happen, if you know how to arrange it.

"I found a reference to something called the Great Mother when I was going through some books the other day. Made me wonder, is that what she thinks she is, my witchy woman spirit friend?

"I only glanced through it, couldn't really be bothered to read it properly. Does she think she's some kind of angel figure or something? Everything has started to get a bit heavier with her after I performed that dark mirror ritual I was working on. Think the thing with the dolls added to it as well.

"It's almost as if I've turned something on, something that I shouldn't have bothered playing with.

"You see, I searched about and managed to find an old mirror in the end. It was stuffed in the back of the old man's wardrobe, all wrapped up in a threadbare blanket. It almost looked as if he had hidden it there on purpose.

"Well, I stood there in my ritual room, with the only light coming from them candles. I stared into that old mirror for what seemed like days. In the end, it was barely a couple of hours, felt like far more though; I seemed to lose a load of time in there.

"Nothing happened at first. It was only when I'd had enough, when I'd decided to give up, that I spotted something right in the corner of the mirror.

"At first it was just a dull smudge. I was going to wipe it off, give it a bit of a polish but then it started moving on its own.

"Slowly, it began to slide from one side of the mirror to the other. Then it stopped and moved back until it settled in the middle. My eyes was hooked on it by that time. Once that smudge reached the middle it stopped and pulsed in front of me. It seemed to be drawing my eyes into it, like a black hole drawing in light. I found I couldn't drag my eyes away.

"Suddenly I realised that I could see someone. It wasn't very clear at first, but it was definitely the figure of a woman.

"I was trying to make sense out of what I was seeing, when I realised that it was a reflection. The figure was actually standing right behind me. Should have thought about that before. Even with that knowledge, I still couldn't drag my eyes away from the mirror. I tried to turn around to see her but I couldn't do it, something held me there, my eyes fixed on hers. That damned witchy woman.

"After a countless period of time, I spotted another figure in the background. It was the old man standing there, I could see him quite clearly. As far as I could tell, he was wearing a gown, something like the one that I had on. There was a forced grim smile on his face.

"He was staring intently at the woman, but she was ignoring him; acting as if he wasn't there. Her whole attention was firmly fixed on me.

"At that moment, the old man seemed to notice that I could see him, and he turned his attention towards me. His mouth moving animatedly, as if he was shouting at me. He seemed to be trying to tell me something but I couldn't hear a damned thing.

"Focusing on his lips, I attempted to read what it was that he was saying, what he was trying to tell me. 'Go for it. Do it. Don't let her stop you.' That was what he seemed to be saying to me. He should have realised that the decision had already been made by that time; I wasn't going to let her get in my way, not now. There was no way that she was going to stop me.

"It was only after that first encounter in the mirror that I started to hear things clearly. It was almost as if I'd switched off the mute button; wish I could turn the fucking thing back on. I heard her voice last night, first time that I've actually heard it with any clarity. It came to me out of nowhere.

"It started off like before, started like a swarm of bees humming in the distance. After a while it changed into some kind of choir of voices, they was all mixed together, one on top of the other. That was when one voice broke through all the noise. One voice stood out from the rest with infinite clarity. When it did, it came at me again and again, countless repetitions of the same phrase.

"'On the night of my ascension, I will stop you.' Yeah, that's what I heard. It went on and on, until finally I had to get out of the house and head to a local bar.

"That voice followed me for a bit, invading my head, banging on like a sick headache. It only stopped when I picked out a real noisy place to have a drink. It was one of them places full of loud monotonous beats; crap to listen to, but at least it drowned out that voice.

"She thinks she can stop me, does she? Well, I'll show her; she ain't stopping me now."

# Eighteen

Mike Dean spent the next two days in Tac's company, day and night. Toni Sillwood saying that she didn't want to run the risk of him trying to disappear from the hotel. She needed plenty of time to continue working on his recovery. During those long days, Mike couldn't help turning his mind back to when he had supported Tac through his heroin problem. The similarities were quite obvious to him. Mentioning those days to Toni, she explained that things like that could leave Tac vulnerable. They could lay in wait, leaving him weak and more open to any outside influences, as was now the case. The state they had found him in didn't seem to be that different to those days. This time though, it looked as if it was far more of a mental problem that they had to crack and less of a physical one.

During those long days, Tac appeared to be living in a strange nowhere state. He often acted as if he was on a different plane of reality to the rest of them. Drifting in and out of logical thought, his subconscious mind would twist everything around in his head. It all became mixed and caused him a great deal of confusion. There were a couple of times, toward the end of the third day, when Tac was close to being his old self again. On those occasions he would sit there chatting to Mike about, music, new staging ideas for the band and how Sam and Cheyenne were doing. A moment later, for no obvious reason, he would drift off into a rambling diatribe that made little or no sense.

Those days were as hard on Mike Dean as they were confusing to Tac. He could detect his old friend's inner torment, it floated across the surface of everything that he said and did. Mike focused all of his attention on trying to help him through it. Richard Levi was invaluable over that time, as he ran off around town on various errands for Toni Sillwood. He would search out suppliers where he could buy the best possible remedies. Toni began each day by talking to Tac. The conversations often continued for a couple of hours, before they came to an end. Leaving the hotel after those meetings, she would then disappear for hours at a time.

Toni Sillwood never said much about where she was going or what she was doing on those trips. When she returned, she would give them little information about what she had been up to. It was all a bit of a mystery as far as Mike was concerned, but he focused his energy on helping Tac and let her get on with what she had to do. The trips left a little bit of a void in proceedings but Richard Levi insisted that they should let her get on with it. He pointed out that Toni would fill them in when she had something to tell them and not before. When she was away, Richard showed that he had a particularly good knowledge of medicine. That was especially when it came to the use of some of the lesser-known herbal treatments. He would sit in his room mixing and brewing potions for ages, like a modern day shaman. For those few days everything that they did was focused on Tac's recovery. Their actions aimed at removing whatever influences were fighting to control him.

The moment that they returned to the hotel with Tac, Toni had set to work on him. She had been able to break through a couple of lower level layers of the force that was holding him without issue. That enabled them to discover that there wasn't another Star of Destiny meeting due for several days. At least that gave them a little bit of leeway, some time to play with. While Mike Dean and Richard Levi worked away in the hotel, looking after Tac, Toni ran off on a number of long trips. She wanted to investigate the significance, if any, of the date when the next meeting was due to take place. She was certain that everything that they were seeing was leading to a specific point. Rites were far more powerful if they coincided with the right planetary alignments.

After some persuasion, Toni Sillwood explained her main aim, before heading off again. She wanted to make contact with a German group that he had heard about. They were like the Union of the Mountain Ash in their ways of working. She was hoping that if she could link up with them, they would be willing to help, if things were to get out of hand. The talisman that she had brought with her would be more than enough to prove her identity and status. First off, she had to find them though, and that was turning out to be far harder than she had anticipated. At one point, Toni spent over twelve hours away from the hotel. In all that time she didn't contact them, which raised Mike Dean's level of uneasiness.

When Toni Sillwood finally returned, she looked tired and mentally drained. Even Richard Levi was becoming worried about what was going on by that time. Over dinner that night, after a rest and a well needed shower, Toni explained what had happened. The news that she had to impart wasn't altogether too encouraging. She had been unable to make any contact with the group that she had been searching for. Although she still believed that she was close, they were so secretive that it was proving far from easy.

By the time that they reached the fourth day,Mike thought that Tac had almost recovered from his ordeal. He was a lot more like his old self. Generally, he was happy and in the most relaxed mood, since they had caught up with him in Goslar. The tormented thoughts that had been clouding his mind, confusing everything, had faded. They were now in the background, having dissipated like a headache. Despite all that he had endured, there was little he could tell them about the Star of Destiny.

Toni was certain that a deep-rooted block still held in his unconscious mind. Something that had been planted there to make sure that he wouldn't be able to talk about anything. Either that, or he had always been well away from any matters of real relevance to what the group were planning. If it was a deep block, Toni didn't want to risk trying to remove it on her own. She was worried about the psychological damage that any wrong move might do. Dislodging such deep-rooted obstructions could take a long time, it needed patience and a some careful probing. She would have to find the right triggers, stumbling into the wrong areas could set off anything in Tac's already fragile mind.

Seeing as Tac's slow recovery now looked as if it was on track, the four of them decided to get out of the hotel for a while. The plan was to take a tour around the local area of Herzberg. It was a chance for them to get a breath of fresh air, having cooped themselves up inside the hotel for so long. There was no rush and they took it easy, strolling through streets in the warm sunshine, taking in the views. As they passed a coffee shop, Tac glanced down at a newspaper that was on an otherwise empty table. Noticing the date with some surprise, he pointed out that Sam and Cheyenne were due to join him that weekend. The original plan had been for him to meet them at his hotel in Hannover. Tac stated that he would have to think about relocating himself in time for their arrival.

When Mike Dean told him that Wendy was going to be coming out with them, he visibly relaxed again. Knowing that they wouldn't be travelling alone eased his mind a little bit. That date had been on Mike's mind for a couple of days and although he had mentioned it to Toni, he had said nothing to Tac. It was another clear sign of how much better he was feeling, that he realised the significance of the date. Sam, Wendy and Cheyenne were due to arrive in Hannover late on the Sunday afternoon. Toni suggested that they wait until Monday morning, before driving over to meet them.

Those extra few hours would give her a little more time to attempt the removal of the last of the influences on Tac's mind. Going with that idea, she asked Mike Dean to call Wendy and explain the situation to her. They didn't want them to worry when they arrived in Hannover to find that they weren't there as had been planned. The idea of not meeting Sam and Cheyenne at the airport, sparked a brief argument. In the end Tac saw the logic behind the plan and agreed, although still with some reluctance. It was only when they sat back that evening that Mike realised that it had been Tac who had first argued the point. He was happy that it was another sign of how much better he had become over the preceding few days.

* * *

On the Monday morning having eaten a light breakfast, Mike Dean and Tac set out for Hannover. It was a little after seven o'clock when they drove away from the hotel. They were both in a buoyant mood as they headed out. The day had all the hallmarks of being hot and steamy. The temperature was rising even at that early hour, giving a hint of the stifling heat to come. The plan was for them to meet up with Sam, Cheyenne and Wendy at the hotel in Hannover. They would drive them back to Herzberg, where they had booked them into the hotel that they were in. Toni Sillwood and Richard Levi decided to stay behind for that trip. They wanted to give the pair of them time on their own with their families. They would all meet up that evening, having booked a table at a local restaurant that they had discovered.

The A7 autobahn was congested with a solid flow of Monday morning traffic. Mike Dean drove through the rising heat of the day, the open windows giving little respite from the temperature. He could sense that it was making people more irritable and impatient than usual. A three car pile-up on the outskirts of Salzgitter, did nothing to help smooth the flow of things. Having had to negotiate the M25 and M1 on countless occasions, Mike didn't take too much notice of the inconvenience. The erratic movement of traffic continued on but at a slower pace. It was something that he had become used to and it was nowhere near as bad as the M25 could be at its worst. Once they passed the site of the accident, the cars having been dragged to the side of the road, the flow of traffic sped up to its normal pace. It didn't take long for the cars to get back up to their usual speed, and they were soon making good time once again.

When they reached the hotel, Mike Dean managed to find a spot in the packed car park and pulled in. They were only a short distance away from the main entrance. As he stepped out of the car in relief, he stretch his stiff legs. The air was barely any cooler outside than it had been in the car. Glancing at his watch, he realised that they were pretty much on schedule. They had been able to make up the time that they had lost negotiating the crash. Walking into the cool, air-conditioned hotel, the first person they noticed was Wendy. She was standing there with her back to them, shouting at the girl in front of her. Mike could tell that she was on the edge of losing her temper with the receptionist.

Wendy was waving her arms around erratically, gestures that Mike knew only too well. It told him that she was becoming distressed and frustrated about something. She was never someone to hold back on her feelings, and was now in full flow. The receptionist was taking the brunt of Wendy's anger and didn't appear to be able to deal with the problem. The language gap was obviously making it harder for both of them, as they tried to get their message across to one another.

"Thank fuck you're here!" Wendy shouted, when she turned round in exasperation. Deciding that she was getting nowhere, she now wanted to find someone else that she could talk to. "Sam and Cheyenne… they, they've gone!" She added, bursting into tears that were born of frustration, as she grabbed hold of Mike's arm.

"What do you mean, they've gone, Wend?" Mike Dean asked, taking her in his arms to try to calm her.

"They, they're just gone… and, and they can't explain it." She answered, waving her arm towards the reception desk. The young girl sitting there looked flustered and unsure of herself.

"Wend, try to tell me what happened."

"I, I nipped out for ten minutes… down to, down to the shop, get, get some fags." Wendy stuttered. As she spoke, Tac stood there staring at her blankly, he appeared unable to take in what he was hearing.

"Yeah, okay, so then what?"

"Cheyenne was in the bath and Sam, Sam was getting dressed."

"Take it easy, Wend." Mike Dean said, realising that she was in danger of losing the plot. She was becoming hysterical, something that he had never seen from her before.

"When I got back." Wendy said, taking a deep breath and grabbing Mike's arm firmly. "When I got back, they, they were gone. There's no sign of them anywhere!"

"Well, they can't have disappeared, they must be somewhere…" Tac said over Wendy's shoulder, he was now starting to look as shaken as Wendy.

"I've been trying to explain it to this asshole but she doesn't seem to understand." Wendy added. She stabbed a bright red fingernail towards the receptionist to emphasise the point.

"Yeah, okay, Wend. Look, do you want to go back up to the room with Tac, see if you can find anything, see if she left a note or anything. My German's a little better than yours, I'll see if I can find out anything." By that time a man in a light blue suit had appeared beside the receptionist and was in deep conversation with her. He glanced up at Wendy as she walked through the foyer, leading Tac towards the lift.

"Hello, I'm the hotel manager." The man said, he didn't offer a name, although he wore a badge stating that he was a Mr Hutton. "Is there a problem here?" His accent and name badge showing that he was not German. In fact, his broad scouse accent told Mike that he came from Liverpool.

"Yeah, our friends seem to have disappeared from their room. We need to find them, it's rather urgent."

"Well, I would guess that they've gone down to the shops or something. I'm sure they'll be back before you know it."

"Look, I'm sorry, but this is rather important. They wouldn't have gone off anywhere, they were expecting us. They knew we were coming."

"You're other friend, there…" He said, waving a hand towards the lift area, as the door slid closed behind Wendy and Tac. "She went out, they could have been following her, trying to catch up with her."

"No, mate. I'm telling you, they wouldn't have gone off like that. They were getting ready for us to arrive. It's not something that they would've done. Could you check to see if anyone saw them leave, or look at your CCTV, you do have CCTV, don't you? There must be something you can do."

"Okay, okay, let's not get over excited here." Mr Hutton said, as he glanced at a group of people heading towards the café area and lowered his voice to a whisper. "If you could wait there for a minute, I'll have a word." He added. With that he disappeared through a door in the panelling behind the reception desk.

Several minutes passed by as Mike Dean stood there in the foyer, becoming more and more frustrated as he glanced at his watch. He waited for the hotel manager to reappear, trying not to show his growing anxiety. When Mr Hutton did return, he came from a different direction altogether. He led Mike to a quieter area away from the foyer, before he was willing to speak. Explaining that he had spoken to one of the hotel's barmen, who had been out on the patio, cleaning the windows of the bar area. The man said that he had seen Cheyenne and Sam leaving, accompanied by two men. That had been around half an hour ago, he stated. The barman had noticed them because Cheyenne reminded him of his own daughter. He also said that they had driven away from the hotel at some speed in a dark blue Mercedes. The barman had seen it parked up close to where he was working, a short distance from the patio area.

That was not the kind of information that Mike Dean wanted to hear at all. Once Mr Hutton had finished his account, Mike asked him if he would go up to the room with him. The manager agreed, although with some reluctance, as if he didn't want to become involved. They took the lift to the third floor in an awkward silence, neither of them sure of what to say. Heading down the corridor, they made their way towards Sam and Cheyenne's room. As he stepped through the open door for the first time, Mike glanced around the room. The first thing that caught his eye was that Sam hadn't taken anything with her when she had left. Her suitcase was still laying open on the bed next to Cheyenne's bright pink Disney Princess case. The clothes inside were still packed and tidy, as if Sam had lifted the lid but had taken nothing out.

Walking into the bathroom, they found that the bath was full and the water still lukewarm. The pile of damp towels laying on the floor beside the sink, looked as if they had been left there in a hurry. Glancing towards Mr Hutton, who stood in the doorway, Mike could see that he was feeling more worried about the situation. He could tell that the manager now believed that something might have happened. Considering the state that Wendy had been in when she came down to confront the receptionist. With everything Mike had told him, he could see that their disappearance didn't make any sense.

When Mr Hutton asked his next question, the answer was a firm no. There was no one that Sam knew in Hannover that she might go off with like that. With some reluctance, the manager agreed that something untoward could have happened. With that in mind, he would be willing to call the local police and get them involved. It was still possible that the car they had left in could be traced. Mike considered the idea for a moment but said that he wanted to make a call himself, before they did anything. Stepping into the corridor he punched out Toni Sillwood's number.

Mike Dean ran through everything that had happened to them since their arrival at the hotel. As he finished, he spotted Tac coming out to the room, Mr Hutton following him into the corridor. They were both looking around, trying to find what Mike was doing. The manager stating that he needed to know what they wanted him to do next, as he had other things to attend to. The last question that Toni asked, when Mike said that he had to go, was how Tac was taking it. She asked whether he was showing any signs of becoming stressed by the events. It was only at that point, that Mike realised how calm Tac was behaving. He appeared to be taking it all in his stride, as if nothing unusual had happened. If it had been him and Wendy had gone missing like that, Mike was sure that he would have been frantic.

Taking Toni's advice, Mike Dean told Mr Hutton that they didn't want to involve the police at that time. They were now going to return to the hotel in Herzberg. Knowing that it was a little unfair, Mike asked Wendy if she would be willing to stay in Hannover, it wasn't something that he was comfortable with, but he couldn't see any other way round it, at that time. Someone needed to be at the hotel in case Sam and Cheyenne were to return. He wasn't happy about Wendy being there on her own, but Tac said that he would stay as well, they could wait for Sam together. Mike decided that it was a good idea and would solve a couple of issues. If nothing else, it would keep Tac away from the Harz Nature Park and any further meetings of the Star of Destiny.

Before he began the return trip to Herzberg, Mike asked Wendy to phone him if anything were to happen. He gave her number for their hotel in case she couldn't reach his mobile. Heading out to the car, he made ready for the return journey on his own. If he waited any longer, he knew he might change his mind about leaving Wendy behind. When he reached Herzberg, after an uneventful drive, he found Toni Sillwood waiting. Standing by the hotel's entrance, she was surprised to see him arriving on his own, when he drove into the car park. Once the situation was explained, she said that she guessed that it couldn't do any harm. As Mike had said himself, at least Tac would be out of the firing line in Hannover.

# Nineteen

A little after two o'clock the next afternoon Wendy phoned through to Mike Dean. A torrential thunderstorm had settled on the area but it did nothing to easy the stifling heat. She had some news for him about what had happened that morning in Hannover. The first bit piece of information that she had to offer came out in a torrent of words, the moment he answered the call. Tac had now also disappeared from the hotel. She explain that he had been acting a little strange ever since they had met up for breakfast. At first, she had put it down to his having a reaction to Sam and Cheyenne's disappearance. Shortly before one o'clock, the time they had arranged to meet up for lunch, she glanced out the window and saw him. Unable to do anything, she watched Tac walk out of the hotel and jump into a waiting taxi.

Not sure what to do, Wendy waited for the best part of an hour, in case he was to return. Under the circumstances, it looked as if that was unlikely to her. Having imparted this latest piece of news, Wendy said that she would now stay on at the hotel on her own. Mike Dean said that he would drive down and pick her up, but she refused the offer. She was willing to stay, in case any of them returned to the hotel, someone needed to be there. Confirming that she would phone Mike back if anything else happened, she said goodbye. With the information rushing around in his head, Mike ran straight up to Toni's room, as soon as he'd finished the call. As the lifts were busy, he took the stairs from the foyer two at a time in his rush to get there. He almost ran straight into an elderly couple that he came across part of the way up the staircase, in his haste.

Toni Sillwood was talking to Richard when Mike entered the room. The moment that he walked through the door, he told them about Tac's disappearance. He quickly added that Wendy had decided to stay put in Hannover. Perching himself on the edge of the bed, he tried not to look worried by the latest development. They all became lost in thought for a time, before Toni said they needed to work out their next move. Clearly they could scour Germany for weeks and have little chance of finding their friends. It would be very fortunate to track them down that way, as they could be anywhere.

The one fact that they had to go on was the Star of Destiny meeting, that was due. That was something solid, something that was growing closer by the hour. Feeling that they had to act, rather than sitting around in the hotel, Mike made a suggestion. They could stake out the area of the cave system in Elbingerode. As that was the site of the earlier meeting, it was the perfect place for them to start. With a little luck, they could find something that they had missed. A vital piece of information must have bypassed them in the chaos. As far as Toni Sillwood could see everything was leading towards an event of some kind. The question was, what kind of an event would that be? She was sure that another meeting must be due soon, especially now that Tac had run off. It all had to be connected, somehow.

With Tac's disappearance, everything was pointing to the fact that something was going to happen. It all had to be a part of it in some way, they just had to discover how. After trying to stay as calm as possible for the afternoon, they sat down to an early meal before setting off. The evening was drawing in when they made their way towards Elbingerode. They passed through the village, that was still damp from the day's incessant downpours.

After the village, they headed to the spot where they had parked up on the first visit to the area. It was well concealed, sitting off the main road, the dense treeline helping to hide the car from any passing traffic.

It was still early in the evening when they arrived at their chosen parking spot. With that in mind, they decided to stay put for a time, not wanting to move too soon. They sat listening to unseen wildlife scurrying around the undergrowth, lost in thought. The passing traffic noise on the main road, came to them through the trees as an occasional faint drone. As time passed they all became a little impatient, wanting to do something. Once it clicked around to nine o'clock, they all decided that it was time for them to make a move. Sitting in the car was making them feel uneasy, the tension growing between them. They were all determined to do something positive. Although by that time there hadn't been any more rain for several hours, the undergrowth was still soaked. The trees dripped on them as they walked along the now muddy trails that they were following. Making the way down the valley, towards the river, they tried not to become engulfed in the thick mud. It congealed around their boots, sucking at them and threatening to envelop them completely.

After what felt like hours of trudging onward, they turned off the main trail and pushed their way into the thicker undergrowth that was surrounding them. With great care, they made for the spot where they had been able to watch the previous meeting. Mike Dean had no idea how Toni could remember the route that they had taken. It wasn't long before they became aware of the faint sound of voices coming to them from off in the distance. That change in atmosphere caused them to become more cautious. Continuing through the dense foliage, they tried to keep as silent as possible. Large growths of bramble scraped at them, roots attempted to trip them up, but they forced themselves on.

Several minutes later, they came to a spot where they could look down on to the cave entrance. They saw a crowd amassed in the clearing below, it was obvious from the first glance that there were far more people there for this meeting. The mixture of punk style and normal clothing was still about the same though. As they watched, there was a relaxed atmosphere hanging over the area, no sign of any tension in the air. The crowd milled around talking and laughing; the meeting not having been underway by that time.

From where he knelt, wet grass soaking into the knees of his jeans, Mike Dean scoured the area. He was searching for any indication that Tac, Sam or Cheyenne where there but there was no sign of them at all. The one person that Mike did recognise straight away was Rick Fischer. Looking over the crowd, he pointed out the unmistakable figure to Toni Sillwood. At the time Rick was standing near to the cave entrance. He was talking to an athletic looking woman, with arms covered shoulder to wrist in tattoos. As he spoke, Rick was pulling an armband over his right shirtsleeve. It matched those being worn by the rest of the crowd.

Once Mike Dean had pointed him out, they all paid close attention to what Rick Fischer was doing. Taking note of the people that he was talking to, they searched for anyone they recognised. The scene changed little over the next half an hour, as the mass of people grew ever larger. There were still regular groups making their way down towards the clearing. Mike's attention was drawn away from the main crowd, when he saw activity near the cave entrance. He pointed out the change to the others, in case they had missed it themselves. They watched Rick Fischer and the man that had been with Tac at the previous meeting, who they now knew to be Hendrik. In a systematic way, the two men cleared a circle of ground in the centre of the area. As they worked, they moved people away to the edges where they congregated in tight groups.

When the section of ground was clear of any obstructions, Rick Fischer began to set out a series of small bricks. The massed crowd of people watched on in silence. From a distance the bricks appeared to be like those that Mike Dean had uncovered during the tour. Rick used them to mark out a large circle on the ground. As he positioned each of the bricks with great care, Hendrik followed him around, placing a thin black candle on top of each one of them. Once the circle had been formed, Rick took a taper out of his pocket and lit the candles one by one. Any noise from the crowd had reduced by that time, and was now little more than a background whisper as people watched the scene playing out before them. With the candles lit, a deeper silence enveloped the area, a sense of anticipation flowing through the gathering.

The candles burnt themselves out as the crowd watched on in awed silence. At that moment six men stepped out of the cave carrying what looked like a large, roughly hewn boulder between them. They struggled to move the load which was hanging in some kind of rope harness strung across their shoulders. Setting the boulder down it in the centre of the circle with great reverence, the men backed out of the circle. It appeared as if they didn't want to be in there any longer than they had to be. Mike Dean noted that none of the men turned their backs on the boulder, backing out of the circle as if it might attack them. Reappearing at the cave mouth, Hendrik carried something wrapped in thick black cloth. He placed his bundle on top of the boulder, stretching across it to reach the centre. As Hendrik unwrapped the cloth, he revealed the figure of Cheyenne adorned in a rich, dark red tunic. She was laying there quite still, as if she were asleep, or to Mike Dean's horrified mind, something worse.

The whole of the site had now gone deathly still, the sense of anticipation palpable, with no one daring to move or speak a word. The tense silence was broken with the sound of chanting coming from a tall muscular man who had stepped out of the cave entrance. He had a great mane of white hair that flowed out across his broad shoulders and cascaded down his back. Mike and Richard crouched in the undergrowth, becoming almost hypnotised by the scene. The drama playing itself out in front of them, as they gazed on. A sense of deep shock was flowing through them both, this was something that they had never dreamt of. Engrossed in what was going on before them, they didn't notice that Toni Sillwood had slid away. When they spotted her, she was creeping towards the back of the massed crowd.

The chanting of the white-haired man rose in its intensity. Despite the silence of the crowd, it was impossible for Mike to work out whether there were any words in the chant. It could have been a pure rhythmic sound, that flowed across the clearing. At that moment, Mike saw Tac stepping into the circle carrying a long, vicious looking dagger in his clenched fists. He was walking in an awkward, uncoordinated way. It looked as if something was trying to stop him from moving, pulling him backward with every step forward that he took. Tac's body movement was all wrong, it was disjointed and unnatural. His eyes were focused on a spot somewhere in front of him, but he didn't seem to be seeing anything. Mike Dean gasped at the sight and turned to speak to Toni Sillwood. That was the moment that he realised that she had left them. She had disappeared into the surrounding bushes in silence. Noticing his sudden movement, Richard grabbed hold of Mike Dean's arm. He pointed to the edge of the clearing that was closest to them. A few yards behind the massed crowd of people, Toni was kneeling on the scrubby grass. As they tried to see what she was doing, she placed her precious flightcase onto the ground. For a moment she crouched over it, making a sign with her hand. The pair watched as, with great reverence, Toni unlocked the case for the first time and lifted the lid. The crush of people in front of her were intent on what was happening before them, and they didn't take any notice.

Toni Sillwood retrieved an object from the case that looked from a distance like a piece of tree branch. As she closed the lid, her lips were moving as she muttered some words over the object. It looked to Mike as if she was praying to it. When she rose to her feet, Toni lifted the foot-long section of branch and held it above her head. With great deliberation, she walked towards the crowd. Once she was amongst the outer few onlookers, she raised her voice above that of the white haired man, chanting to the crowd. Even from a distance her voice reached Mike and Richard, they could clearly hear every word.

"You will stop this abomination!" She said, as her voice was picked out by everyone in the crowd and the mass of people turned towards her.

Toni Sillwood's intervention changed the scene into one of chaos. The angry throng moved in her direction, wanting to discover what was disrupting the meeting. Mike Dean was now on his feet, no longer worried about the crowd seeing him, he watched what was going on intently. He was wondering if there was any way that he could help Toni before the mob turned on her. The idea of concealment was long gone, as he tried to force his way through the bushes to get down to her. After a few moments he realised that something strange was playing out before him. For some reason the attacking crowd were unable to get close to Toni. She strolled through them, like a knife through butter, unheeded by grasping hands and other obstacles that appeared in her way.

At that moment, Mike Dean saw a large rock that had been flung towards her, from somewhere at the back of the crowd. The missile seemed destined to strike Toni full on the head, but when it was a couple of feet away from her, it stopped dead in the air and fell impotently to the ground. That was the final straw, the crowd as one began to panic, rushing off in all directions. They weren't worried where they were heading, as long as it was away from Toni. As Mike watched the crowd running to escape the area, he noticed a dark shadow that was pushing its way through the mob. There was no real shape to the shadow, it was an indistinct absence of light flowing out of the cave entrance, but he could see that people were cowering away from it.

Toni stood her ground between the shadowy mass and the boulder where Cheyenne was laying. The darkness inched forward, like a stalking animal it moved from one side to the other, but Toni kept her position, eyes following its every motion. Slowly the mass of darkness took on a shape. Although indistinct and shadowy, it formed into that of a panther-like cat, its glowing red eyes the only colour in the blackness. As the creature reared up, looking as if it was about to pounce, Toni changed her grip on the talisman and swung it viciously at the apparition. The talisman met the dark head and there was a clap of thunderous noise followed by a blinding flash of light. Mike had been looking directly at the creature and his eyes were unable to see anything for a moment, as a result of the intensity of the flash. As his vision cleared, he saw that the creature had disappeared. Toni was standing there, massaging her arm as if in pain, but then she turned towards the boulder.

Approaching the silent figure of Cheyenne, Toni stepped straight past Tac. He was still standing there within touching distance of his daughter. He was not moving, like a marble statue, the dagger clenched in his unmoving hands. Toni Sillwood placed her free hand on Cheyenne's chest for a couple of moments. Channelling her energy towards the girl, she waited until she showed signs of stirring. Tac hadn't moved a muscle during all that time. Reaching over, Toni grabbed the blade that he was holding, snatching it away in one sharp movement. With the dagger now in her hands, she stuck the blade into a crack in the boulder and in one quick motion, snapped it in half. The blade broken, she threw the pieces onto the ground and kicked them out of her way. At that moment Tac appeared to wake up. He looked around the now calm, deserted clearing in a daze. Glancing down, he saw Cheyenne laying on the boulder, wrapped in the red gown. She had trying to push herself up into a sitting position. As far as Mike could see, Tac hadn't even seen her until that moment.

Within a few minutes, tears were pouring down his face, threatening to engulf him. He staggered over towards his daughter, ignoring Toni by his side. Reaching across, he folded the black cloth around her, pulling her to his chest and holding her there, his arms wrapped around her protectively. Cheyenne's long dark hair rolled over Tac's shoulder as he held onto her. With the slow passage of time, she became more and more aware of where she was, trying to take in her surroundings. At that moment there was a cry from inside the cave. A few seconds later Sam came running out of the entrance, wrapping her arms around the two of them.

Mike Dean and Richard Levi made their way down into the clearing as fast as they could. They had been watching the episode playing out before them, like the scene from some bizarre film. Neither of them sure what they had witnessed but at least the outcome seemed to be a positive one. Toni stepped back over to her flight case, which was still laying on the ground where she'd left it. Picking it up, she carried it to the nearby boulder. Flicking open the catches, she placed the branch onto the rich velvet bed, securing two straps to hold it. Before she closed the lid, Toni removed three green shoots that were growing on the side of the branch. Handing Tac, Sam and Cheyenne a shoot each, she told them to keep them close. She went on to explain that they would protect them from any negative influences.

They could all tell that Tac was feeling confused by the events of the evening. He didn't seem to know what had happened, what he had been involved in. The first question that he asked Mike, as he reached his side, was where they were. It seemed as if he had never seen the cave entrance before. Tac became even more shaken up when Sam explained that they were in Germany. He had no clear memory of having travelled there at all. In fact, he said that he thought they were still somewhere in the UK. Since the departure of the Star of Destiny, the area outside the cave had taken on an air of peacefulness and calm. That was in direct opposition to what it had been like a short time before.

"So, what was that?" Mike Dean asked. He had watched Toni Sillwood close the lid of the flight case, concealing the contents from view.

"Not now, Mike, I'll try to explain things to you all later." Toni said, adding. "Now's not the time to get into that."

"Yeah, I guess so."

"We need to clear things up here, before anything else."

"Well, what do you need me to do now?"

"For now, I want to cleanse this area, the best that I can. Then we should get out of here."

"Okay, is there anything I can do to help?"

"Best thing you can do right now, Mike. Go back and fetch the car, I don't think Cheyenne would be able to make it that far, or Tac for that matter."

"Yeah, I'm on it. Be back as soon as I can."

"Oh, and Mike. Keep an eye out for anyone that might still be hanging around, we can't be sure that they've all run off." Toni Sillwood warned, as Mike made his way off into the treeline.

With Mike Dean disappearing into the distance, Richard Levi made his way over to Cheyenne. He wanted to make sure that she had not come to any harm in any way. While he was checking her over, Toni Sillwood looked around the site. She was studying the layout of the circle of bricks and their alignments to each other, trying to take in the scene. As they had seen Rick Fisher set them out with such care, she was certain that there had to be some meaning to it all. The mixture of astrological and Cabbalistic signs were ones they had already encountered. Mixed in with them, Toni found a few new figures, scattered around amongst the circle of bricks. Taking a scrap of paper out of her pocket, she got down on her knees and started making notes. Mapping out the positions of the various signs, she looked for how each one fitted with others. It wasn't long before she was able to work out the basic structure of the circle. She went on to explain that it would take time to glean any deeper meanings out those alignments.

With her sketching of the circle finished, Toni Sillwood searched around the clearing. She hunted through the accumulation of debris that had been left behind by the crowd. Finding an empty lemonade bottle, she picked it up with two plastic carrier bags that were on the ground. Filling the bags with bricks, she swung them against the cave wall, crushing them into a gritty rubble. They were so brittle that it didn't take much effort for her to demolish them. Once the bricks had been destroyed, Toni took the bags down to the nearby river and emptied the contents into the fast-flowing water. The free running water would dissipate any last vestiges of power that the bricks might hold. Toni told Richard that free running water was always a good cleanser, as he stood watching her.

Rinsing the lemonade bottle that she had found, Toni Sillwood then filled it with fresh water. She carried the bottle over to where her flight case was standing beside the boulder. Lifting the talisman out once again, she carefully turned it around in her hands. Snapping off several of the green shoots that were growing on it, she crushed them in the palm of her hand. Dropping the shoots into the bottle of river water, Toni swirled the mixture around for a few moments, she then put it down on the ground to let it settle. Richard Levi watched in fascination, as the mixture turned a faint milky colour. Toni returned the talisman to its case and locked it again, while the bottle rested. After some time, she turned her attention back to the bottle, waiting for the water to clear. The mixture had now become completely transparent, any sign of cloudiness gone.

Toni held the bottle up to the bright moonlight that was

forcing its way through the light cloud cover. She spent several minutes studying the contents. The water had now become even clearer than it had been, there was now a crystalline quality to it. Walking to the centre of the circle, she chanted a few words. Although unintelligible to the others, they all agreed that it felt like an ancient language. When she had finished her chant, she sprinkled the clean water over the area. She was paying particular attention to the section of ground where the bricks had been placed.

With the bottle empty, the water soaking into the ground, Toni Sillwood tossed it away. It joined the rest of the debris that cluttered the ground where the crowd had been standing. Picking up her precious flight case, she called everyone together. There was nothing else for them to do, she said, so they should start making their way up the main track to the road. Mike Dean should have recovered the car by that time, as long as he'd had no problems, and would be on his way towards them. They would meet him at the top of the trail, where it would be easier for him to pick them up. Everyone was more than happy to escape the area by that time, and they all agreed.

Tac picked Cheyenne up, she was still looking a little dazed, and they didn't think that she would be able to walk very far. As they passed her, Toni Sillwood draped her jacket over Cheyenne's shoulders. Both Sam and Cheyenne were visibly shivering in the cooling night air. Though the evening was not yet too cold, they were aware that the temperature would soon change. By that time a mixture of shock and relief was flowing over them all. That was more to do with their reaction to what had happened rather than the temperature. Making their way straight up the main track, they reached the road without meeting anybody. A few minutes later,

Mike appeared in the distance, heading towards where they were standing.

# Twenty

"Well, it seems as if my suspicions were right all the time. Course, I usually am right about these things, ain't I?

"That Toni woman and Tac's mate have come over here to meddle in my affairs.

"Guess they want to try and stop me! Why the fuck's everyone trying to stop me? Why can't they all leave me alone?

"The moment I was told about their arrival, I had a feeling that might be the case. Especially when I heard about them being rushed through the airport like that. Not normal that, not the way things usually work.

"Still it's too late for me to do anything about them now. They don't know what they're up against, they can't have any idea; they don't know me at all.

"Things are getting far too close to completion now. Can't allow them to distract me, get in my way. I need to concentrate on everything, make sure I get it all right.

"They managed to disrupt the ritual last night. They turned the whole fucking thing into chaos. Them bloody Star of Destiny bastards were a useless bunch of losers in the end, as I always thought they would be, if it came to it. Soon as that Toni woman turned up like that, waving that thing at them, they all ran off like scared little children.

"Had to conjure up that demon creature, so I could get away. Never done anything like that before, the idea just came into my head out of nowhere. Worked really well that did. Bit more practice and that could be a really powerful creature to play with.

Could use it in all sorts of places.

"Suppose I shouldn't be too surprised about the Star bods though, should I? That was always likely to happen. Kinda knew I wouldn't be able to rely on them. I can't afford to rely on anyone. They all turned and ran for their miserable lives, first sign of something they didn't understand. First sign that there was a problem.

"Course I could have taken her on, could have beaten her but things are too close now. I couldn't afford to risk that, can't afford to jeopardise it when I'm so close.

"Thought I might be able to rely on one or two of them. Thought they might have some balls. Micha seemed to be pretty on it when I talked to her, don't know about all them bloody tattoos though! Still, wouldn't let that put me off her, if I got the chance.

"Then there was that Javier bloke. Well, he came over as a pretty cold and silent kinda bloke, I like that, can understand it. Thought he might be able to add something, but he proved me wrong. Meant to have been in a couple of paramilitary groups in the past, so I heard. Didn't act very paramilitary out there, did he?

"How wrong can you be? Took off like the devil his self was after him. Well, they'll soon find out what that feels like, once I've finished my little ritual.

"Course a lot of them wanted to get to know me, wanted to talk to me, but I ignored most of them. Right tossers most of them. Still, a couple of them managed to amuse me for a little bit.

"Worst thing about last night was losing the chance to get the blood that I was after. Had Tac all programmed for that one, another fifteen minutes and I would have had it. Her blood taken by her father? Oh yeah, that would have been good, that would.

"I'll make them pay for messing that one up for me. They'll all pay, specially that Toni bitch, coming over here, sticking her nose in like that. Oh, she'll pay!

"Well, I'll have to make do, won't I? Bit of improvisation, but I'm getting good at that. Tac's daughter's blood would have been a rather special addition to the whole thing but that's gone now. No use crying about it. At the end of the day, blood's blood. Yeah, one might be a little bit better than another, but it's all red when you come down to it. I can get as much as I want.

"Guess I'll have to do without having them Star bods hanging around now, well, fuck them, I can do without them. I don't need them anymore, they've served their purpose.

"At least I've still got my hard-core group. Might not be too many of them left, but they'll do what I want them to do, no questions asked.

"Think I'll have to make use of Cillian, if I'm going to have to lose one of them.

"Yeah, Cillian it is. He's pretty weak, not much use for anything else, he can be useful and provide the blood that I'll need. Have to do that myself, can't rely on any of the others to do it for me and I don't want them to start running scared.

"If Cillian happens to disappear over-night, none of them will think anything of it. They'll just think he's run off, got scared, couldn't handle it any more. He wouldn't be first to run off like that.

"Right now, I've got to focus on Friday, and the full moon. The timing is perfect. That will be the ideal time for me to bring this whole thing off. Then I won't need any of those hangers-on, they can all fuck off and leave me, see if I care.

"Don't want to have to wait any longer, not with that Toni woman running around. The next full moon is far too distant, too many things could go on before then.

"I'll bring Baphomet here, I will stand beside him, and we will be all powerful. No one will be able to stop us then.

"I can't help thinking about the things that we could do together, the things we could manage. It all keeps buzzing through my head. Puts a shiver down my spine that does. Thinking about all the power that I'll be able to unleash, all the things that we could do together.

"I will be supreme! I will dominate this world; people will cower before me!

"Need to hold back a little bit though, mustn't allow myself to get too carried away. It ain't done yet. There's still a lot for me to do, if it's all going to work out. Can't start thinking that it's all in the bag, all done and dusted. That's how people make mistakes, that is.

"It seems as if I've been able to silence that damned witchy woman, or spirit, or whatever the fuck she thinks she is. Since that doll ritual I performed, I've seen little of her. I've checked in my mirror a couple of times, and she's still there. Still trussed up like some damned mummy, fucking good that is, real good.

"Course I knew I could pull it off, all I had to do was persevere, keep at it. If you don't succeed at first, do it again and again. Refine and adapt; that's always the best way, that is.

"Don't trust her though. I know she still wants to stop me, and she will, if she can find a way to do it. Damned sure I ain't going to let her though, ain't going to give her the chance, I can tell you that for nothing. When I have Baphomet beside me, I'll banish her to whatever spirit witchy world she came from. She won't trouble anyone ever again, I'll make damned sure of that.

"Bit of a pain losing all those Star bods, I must admit.

"Was planning to use them to cause a little disturbance on Friday afternoon. Thought that if I set up a little something. A mini riot or an explosion or something like that. Well, it would draw any attention away from me. A bit of a safety measure that would have been, just trying to cover all the angles.

"With that Toni woman and Mike hanging around, I might need to sort out a little distraction. I don't think they've got too much of a handle on what I'm up to though. Don't see how they can have. Soon be over, then it'll be too late for them to do anything about it.

"I don't see how they're likely to find the house, not in time anyway. There shouldn't be anything to lead them in that direction. I've got things pretty tied up here, covered all the bases.

"Course, I know Tac's been there, but it was only the once. He didn't see anything and I've had him all wrapped up, I doubt he even knew what planet he was on at the time. No, can't see a problem there, even if he did wake up a bit. He'd never be able to find it again, let's face it, all the houses look the same round here.

"We have to keep a bit of a low profile for a couple of days, then it'll all be done and dusted. I need some time to prepare everything anyway. Time to cleanse the room ready for the ritual and I'll have to purify myself too.

"Gotta make sure the other four are purified too, course they won't understand what's going on. Not as much as they think they do, anyway.

"Oh, I can't wait for this, you know. This is going to be awesome!

"This will crown me as the greatest black magician the world has ever seen.

"Yeah, Crowley, LaVey and the rest of them, they can all fuck off. I'm far beyond anything they ever thought of, none of them did anything like what I'm going to achieve.

"Was thinking, I could start my own church, like LaVey did. Yeah, the Church of Baphomet, how's that sound?

"I'm planning on setting my mirror up in the room too, want to keep an eye on things. If that bitch is still floating around in there, I want to make sure that she sees everything. There's the old man too, of course, I've seen him in the mirror. It wouldn't be fair to exclude him, especially as he started all this in the first place.

"Yeah, the bastard led me by the nose, now I'll show him what I can do. I'll make him proud of me."

# Twenty-One

The company were late getting up the next day. They were all feeling exhausted and sapped of strength when they had gone to bed. The previous night's events had drained them of most of their energy resources. It had left them feeling subdued and struggling to start the day. They had all been extremely fatigued when they returned to the hotel that night. It was one o'clock in the afternoon by the time that they all managed to meet up in the hotel's lounge. As was often the case, it was Richard Levi who was the last one to make an appearance.

Over a late breakfast of coffee and sweet pastries, Toni Sillwood began to explain everything as far as she could. She ran through all that they had seen the previous night and tried to explained what she thought it had all meant. The initial topic of Toni's attention centred around the shadowy creature that she had faced, which she described as being some kind of demon-like apparition. Unsure of what it actually was or where it had come from, Toni said that the power it held had been intense. She had been able to sense that it was infused with evil, an evil so strong that it had been almost overpowering. The strength of the creature had been unexpected, and her arm was still aching from striking it.

From the creature, Toni moved on to the symbols that she had found on the bricks. She believed that those bricks and how they aligned were of prime importance. One of the main things that still puzzled her was the date of the meeting. It didn't seem to make any sense, it just didn't seem to fit in with anything else that they had uncovered. There was nothing special about the date, as far as she could see, other than it being a full moon. On a large sheet of paper Toni had copied out the rough sketches that she had made the night before. She had drawn connecting lines and several notes to show how everything was linked together.

Toni Sillwood tried to show how the symbols that they had already come across, samekh and aein fitted in. They were in positions that would work in harmony with each other and a third symbol, the planet Mars. Those three forces could be very strong when linked together like that, she explained. Aligned in the way that she had found them, they would work to create an atmosphere of aggression. They would generate greater levels of instability. Phé and noun, the other two symbols that Mike Dean had seen on the unused bricks, were also there. They were also in the circle, but put in positions of opposition.

The symbols of Phé and noun, were placed in areas that Toni Sillwood described as unhelpful. They were square to other bricks that held the signs for the planets Jupiter and Venus. As far as she could tell, they were forces that could have disrupted the influence of evil. Placed in inharmonious positions, they would more likely to be fighting against each other. Set as they were, they would be trying to pull themselves apart, rather than adding any positivity. Their potential powers for good would be fighting the unstable atmosphere that they found. That would leave the negative forces to run free and create chaos.

Toni Sillwood spent the best part of an hour running through the meanings of the various symbols. She explained the importance of each one and how they were being used to work together. Mike Dean sat there listening to everything Toni had to say, but his mind was spinning out of control. He had a host of other questions that he wanted to ask. The moment that Toni came to the end of her explanations, Mike had to jump straight in.

He asked the one question that he couldn't get out of his head. He wanted to discover more about the mysterious talisman. It was sitting in her case, which was on the floor beside her, only inches from them all.

The more he ran through the events of the previous evening in the back of his mind, the less he was able to find an explanation. He couldn't understand the reaction when Toni Sillwood had approached the crowd. As far as Mike could see, Toni had been wielding a piece of the branch of a tree. It was one that still had new shoots sprouting from it, even though it was securely in a locked case. The whole episode was a mystery, it didn't make any sense to him. It was clear to everyone that Toni was uneasy talking to them about the subject. She didn't want to tell them too much about the talisman.

Now Mike Dean had brought the subject up, Toni realised that the rest of the group would be wanting some answers too. They were all keen to learn more about the experience that they had been subjected too. Under the circumstances, Toni Sillwood knew that she couldn't justify keeping quiet. Regardless of what the Union of the Mountain Ash's inner circle had told her that she could do. The rules they had instructed her to observe would now have to be put to one side. She could tell that saying nothing would create turmoil within the group and that would put her in a tough position. She owed them some kind of an explanation. Trying to gloss over it all wouldn't be fair and it would only go to disrupt the harmony of the group. They were all a part what had been going on, they deserved to be fully informed about what they were facing. Taking a deep breath, Toni took some time to refill her cup with rich dark coffee. Resigned herself to giving them a summary of the talisman's history and its potential power, she glanced around the room once again.

"The talisman that you all saw last night." Toni Sillwood said, after taking a mouthful of her coffee and trying to compose herself. "It is a small piece believed to have come from the root of Yggdrasill, the world tree."

"I think I've heard something about that." Mike Dean said, scouring his memories for the source. He couldn't help thinking that it was something from a film that he had recently watched but wasn't at all sure.

"This is something sacred to us in the Union of the Mountain Ash. It represents the cycle of birth, growth, death and rebirth."

"Still think it sounds like something out of a Thor comic!" Mike Dean said, only partially in jest.

"They say that Yggdrasill has three main roots." Toni Sillwood continued, ignoring Mike's comment. "The talisman is a part of the first root, the one that reaches down to the world of the gods. The runic characters carved into its body are said to have been shaped by the gods themselves. That is what gives it its power."

"I know what I saw last night, Toni, but this sounds… oh, I don't know, unreal, ridiculous, bizarre? Take your pick, I, I don't know what to think."

"I realise it's a lot to take in, Mike. I can only tell you what I've learnt myself, it's something that I've come to believe in."

"Okay, Toni. I'm sorry, I don't mean to make light of it." Mike Dean said. He realised that Toni Sillwood was starting to take offence at his reaction. "Please, tell us a bit more about it."

"The talisman of Yggdrasill is powerful; it can only be used in the most extreme of circumstances. I could never have beaten that creature, last night, without it. That was a meeting of light and dark at its most intense. Under normal circumstances it would never leave the vaults of the Union. I felt from the start that this was all leading in bad direction. I argued that something powerful, like the talisman, would have to come into play. It still took a lot of debate amongst the council of the inner circle before they agreed to let me bring it. It's a great honour for them to entrust me with the talisman, few people have had that privilege. It goes to show how strongly the council thought about the things that you brought to our attention, Mike."

"So, Toni, do you know anything about this group that were out there last night." Tac asked, having sat through everything that she had said up till that point without a word.

"Well, on the surface of it, the Star of Destiny seem to be some kind of white extremist group…"

"I'm sure I saw other faces there last night, they weren't all white!" Tac said.

"No, you're quite right, Tac. That's why I'm sure that this group's a bit of a cover for something else. How many of them actually know what's going on in their name, I couldn't even guess."

"So, what do you think they're up to then?"

"Well, underneath it all we are sure they're working for something best described as the left-hand path. I must say that is a rather old, inaccurate label though. If you were to stick with that idea, I suppose you could call what we're doing as working for the right-hand path. It's a loose description for an overriding concept of, and I hate using the word, but evil. At least, I suppose that is the best description to use. No one else would be able to call on something like that creature we saw, it would have taken someone very powerful to conjure that up."

"Does that mean anything, Toni? Left path, right path, it all sound very vague."

"Well, to us those ideas are rather inaccurate too. I was trying to use ideas that you might have come across. At the Union we see everything working more in a circular motion. If you take the extreme path around any circle, left or right, you'll come to the same point in the end, won't you?"

"Surely, if you go by that idea, your views and this Star of Destiny's ideas are the same!"

"There are similarities, I admit that, Mike." Toni Sillwood said, adding. "But our fundamental aims are both very different."

"But how does this affect the talisman that you were telling us about?"

"What you all saw last night was the power of the ancients. It was drawn through and amplified by the talisman of Yggdrasill, that was a small sign of what it can do."

"Toni, I can't help feeling that this whole thing is far from over." Richard Levi stated.

"You say that this isn't over yet." Tac echoed, after a few minutes of tense silence had flooded over the table. "I'm pretty sure that you're right about that."

With those words, Tac became aware that everyone was now looking at him. They all had expectant expressions on their faces, they were curious about how he saw the situation. Tac proceeded to explain that he had suffered a series of disturbing dreams, throughout the night. Those dreams had been so strong and vivid that he could have sworn that they had been real. That he had actually been there. It was only the fact that he had woken up in the hotel, with Sam beside him, that had convinced him they were dreams. The one common image running through all those dreams, he explained, was Rick Fisher.

Rick Fischer was constantly following him around as he made his way down a series of dense, dark streets. After having Rick trail him through the streets, he ended up walking into a building. Tac said that he was sure he recognised that building, although he couldn't place it. The more he recalled the building, as he spoke about it, the more certain he was sure that it was somewhere near to the centre of Goslar. Tac was pretty sure that he had visited the building at some point. Although he did admit that somehow it appeared fundamentally different in his dream. That confusion was worse as he only had vague memories of his time since arriving in Germany.

Encouraged to try to remember more details by Toni Sillwood, Tac sat back in silence for a few minutes. He tried to organise his thoughts, put them in a logical order. When he was ready, he continued by telling them about the things that he had seen Rick Fisher doing in his dreams. The whole of the action focused around him performing some kind of a rite. As far as Tac could see, the activity centring on a small table or bench, cloaked in thick black cloth. Throughout the scene, Rick Fischer was always in a position that obscured Tac's vision. It was impossible to see what was happening on the table. The only light in that dingy basement room, came from a dozen large black candles. They had been placed at regular spaces around the area. The flickering candles made it hard to see clearly, as deep shadows bounced off the walls. It was a surreal scene, one that invoked nightmare visions in the back of his mind.

Tac continued telling them all about the images that he had seen in his dreams. Everything flowed out in an unstoppable stream of consciousness, once he started talking. The moment he finished, gasping for breath, Toni Sillwood said that she was sure that it was far more than a dream. It could be a premonition of some sort, she explained, maybe an omen of things to come. Toni considered everything that he had been through, whether he remembered them or not. It was clear that he had been involved in some of the things that the Star of Destiny had been working on. With the influence of the talisman, Toni was sure that their power over him had now reduced to a degree. That was the reason he was able to focus his mind more on Rick Fisher. It was now clear that he was a high-ranking member of the Star of Destiny or whatever group was behind them.

Tony Sillwood was sure that they should feel encouraged by the things that Tac had now been able to tell them. She suggested that they should take advantage of the slim lead that they had found. Tac was still sure that he would be able to recognise the building again, if he were to come across it. The problem was that he couldn't tell them exactly where they would find it. Before they made the next move, Toni asked Richard Levi to drive Sam and Cheyenne up to the hotel in Hannover. Meeting up with Wendy, they could book themselves into another hotel, well away from the centre of the city. Once they had seen them off, the rest of the group prepared for a drive around Goslar. They were hoping that Tac would see something that could spark off a memory for him. They were looking for anything that would help them to locate the building at the centre of his dreams. With luck, they would be able to put an end to the situation and join up with the others in Hannover.

# Twenty-Two

The roads through to Goslar proved to be reasonably empty and the drive was trouble free. The light traffic moved lethargically in the warm summer's afternoon. Once they were close to the centre of the town, Toni Sillwood pulled out a map of the area. She pointed to the station, as they had come across Tac there. As Hendrik had left Tac in that area, Toni decided that it should be the starting place for their search. From there they slowly drove around the surrounding streets. They were hoping the building they were looking for would be somewhere in that vicinity. As Tac had been left to his own devices, near the station, so it was the logical place to start. He had already told them that the room where he had been staying, above a bakery, wasn't the place they were looking for.

Nothing that they saw, as they toured the streets, sparked any memories for Tac. After an hour of fruitless searching, they turned their attention to a wider area. At first, they headed towards the western side of the town. At one point, Tac said that he had a feeling that the building they were looking for was in the rough direction of the old castle. That building stood on the outskirts of town, where the houses were generally a lot older. It seemed as if they had been driving around for hours without the slightest sign of success. Toni Sillwood was becoming hypnotised by the constant dull noise of the traffic. She was close to suggesting that they should give up and head back to the hotel. They had travelled up and down identical looking streets, getting nowhere, for ages.

Suddenly Mike Dean snapped to attention, he'd seen something at the roadside that had grabbed him. Taking everyone by surprise, he asked Toni Sillwood to pull the car over to the side of the road. He was certain that he'd seen the faint figure of a woman, a radiant light pulsing around her, causing her to look as if she was glowing. He didn't want to tell the rest of them what he had seen, fearing that they would think him mad. The image reminded him of the blur of light that had led him to Rick Fischer's flight case, that day on the tour coach. The order to pull over had come as a bolt from the blue. Toni found herself unable to get out of the flow of traffic with such short notice. Her sudden braking had caused several cars behind her to hit their horns in anger, as it was. Taking the first turning that she came across, she turned away from the main road. Driving around the quieter backstreets, she managed to find a parking space and pulled into it.

Stepping out into the muggy air, they followed Mike Dean along the tree-lined pavement. He strolled off ahead of them, eager to get round to where he had seen the woman. He came to a stop in front of an unremarkable, shabby looking building. It seemed identical to all its neighbours on either side of the street. The moment that they reached it, Tac told them that he recognised it. He was certain that it was the building that he had seen in his dreams and asked how Mike knew about the house. Still not comfortable in saying anything about the woman, Mike muttered an explanation. He said that something in the street had grabbed his attention. Although they were all looking at him in a strange manner, he didn't feel that he could tell them the truth.

There were no signs of life in the street, other than a stray cat scratching at the foot of a nearby tree. The whole area appeared to be peaceful, if anything far too peaceful for Mike Dean's liking. It was like an omen of something happening and it wasn't a feeling that he was very happy with. Nodding towards an alleyway, further down the street, Tac took over and led them to the back of the building. They could see that something had clicked in his mind, he now knew exactly where he was heading. They came to an unremarkable door, covered in flaking green paint and with rusting hinges. Reaching up, he pulled a metal box from its hiding place behind a waste pipe. Opening the lid, he pulled out the key that was sitting inside. In explanation, he said that he remembered seeing Rick Fisher doing the same thing. It was all hidden somewhere amongst his murky memories of past events. He hadn't been sure whether it was part of his dreams or not, but everything was now coming true.

The key fitted into the well-oiled lock without a problem. The lock was the only part of the door that looked new, and the key turned without making a sound. Pulling the door towards him, he expected a screech from the rusty hinges but the silence continued. The opening revealed the dark interior of the building. Stepping into the silent passageway, they closed the door behind them. They walked past a doorway which led into an empty, sterile looking kitchen, and they moved on. There was no sign of life, as they made their way towards the door at the end of the passageway. Pushing the door open, Tac led them into the building's main hallway. They could see three other closed doors and a staircase ahead of them, leading up into the darkness above. Tac said that he remembered being in a room up on the next floor, having spent an evening there.

As Tac was talking, he led them towards the flight of stairs. At that moment, Mike Dean noticed a pulsing light to the right of the staircase. He could tell that no one else could see it, but Mike was now sure that they should follow it. Knowing that he owed them some form of explanation, he told the group why he was sure that they should go that way. Telling them about the glowing woman and how she had led him towards the house in the first place. That was his main reason for wanting to follow where the light was directing him. So far following that glow hadn't let him down, in fact it had helped in many ways. Strolling past the stairs, their footsteps were well muffled by the thick pile of the dark red carpet. Leading the way to the far end of the hall, Mike stopped at an ominous looking door. Explaining that he was certain that this door would lead down to the basement, Mike felt strangely reluctant to touch it. The room that Tac remembered from his dream, would be there, he couldn't say how he knew it, but he was certain of the fact.

They stood there beside the door for several minutes. In awe they tried to take in the hideous, ornate carvings that adorned the wooden panels. The carved figures appeared to move of their own volition in the torchlight. They listened for signs that there were other people in the house but the silence continued. It made them all feel edgy and uncomfortable, a sense of threat hanging over them. Although no one said it, they knew they were preparing themselves for what might come. They could all sense that something was about to happen. Finally glancing at the tense faces of Toni Sillwood and Tac, Mike Dean focused on the next step. The repulsive dwarf-like figures danced in front of him as he took hold of the handle. Turning it with care, he pulled the door towards him and felt it's smooth glide. Revealed behind it was a flight of stone steps that were dank and inhospitable.

The staircase that Mike Dean had exposed was dark and threatening. There was an atmosphere about the place that he had never encountered before. A sensation of malevolence hung over the area, as they inched their way down the bare stone steps.

Hardly daring to breath, they had all become aware that they needed to show extreme caution. Holding the cold metal handrail, Toni Sillwood felt prickles of rust grazing her hand. She led the way down into the depths, having taken the lead without a second thought. After a dozen or so steps, they became aware of the sound of voices drifting up towards them. They were chanting to a steady throbbing rhythm.

Reaching out her hand, Toni Sillwood touched the roughly plastered wall, it left a chalky dust on her fingers. A ghostly glow led them down towards the dim light that was emanating from below. When they arrived at the foot of the stairs, they found a room set out exactly as Tac had portrayed it, it was the one he had described from his dream. The only light in the gloom came from the twelve large black candles that sputtered in the darkness. They gave off an intense aroma, one that threatened to turn their stomachs. The candles were around four feet in height, thick as a tree trunks, and they stood in ornate wrought iron stands. They seemed to writhe like a pit of snakes in the flickering light.

Staring through the darkness, they could make out four shapes standing in front of them. Shrouded in floor length deep red gowns, the figures looked as if they were consuming the candlelight. They were gathered at the far end of the room and had their backs to Toni. The three closest to them stood in silence, their heads bowed in an attitude of reverence. They had their arms held out from their sides, palms turn forward. The figure furthest away from them, arms held high in the air, was chanting in a long monotonous drone. A thick billowing plume of grey smoke was rising in front of him in a greasy threatening way. Suddenly the lead figure moved to one side, as he waved his arms in an unpleasant motion. His movement revealed a squat shape sitting cross-legged on top of a black draped table.

The figure that appeared in the dull flickering light of the candles, could only have come from a bad dream. It was something that would give anyone nightmares. It was a vision that once seen, could never leave one's mind. The creature that sat on the table was dwarfish in stature. It had pale grey skin that seethed in an unhealthy way, as if the skin itself was alive with movement. A sickly-sweet aroma drifted through the room, carried on the smoke that shrouded the figure. That smoke made Mike Dean feel like throwing up, as he stared at the creature. He was becoming lost in the horror and disgust of what he was seeing. The lingering smell threatened to turn all of their stomachs.

The nightmare creature sat there before them fingering its erect, grossly deformed penis. Its large bloated breasts appeared to be leaking a greenish poisonous looking fluid. Worse than the creature's body, was the top-heavy and unstable head, which sat on its gnarled shoulders. The creature had a head that looked like a goat's but it was unlike any goat that any of them had ever seen before. They could see two ivory horns sticking out of its course, dark red fur. The beady black eyes radiated an intense aura of evil, as it tried to scour the room myopically. It was aware that something wasn't right, that someone was there that shouldn't be.

The creature realised there were people in the shadows at the back of the room, people who shouldn't have been there. Whether it could see them through its staring eyes, was impossible to tell. Alerted to their presence, the four shrouded figures turned towards the group. The three nearest to them stepping forward, waving vicious looking daggers in the air. The one who stood beside the creature, shouting that they would pay for their intrusion. As the candlelight flickered across his face, they all recognised Rick Fischer.

The three men charged across the room with their daggers poised to strike. Dark red cloaks streaming out behind them like flames. At that moment, Toni Sillwood pushed past Mike Dean and Tac. Once again, she was brandishing the talisman of Yggdrasill in front of her. When their attackers saw the talisman, the three men cowered back. There was a look of panic in their eyes, as the power emanating from the talisman flowing around the room in surges. Staggering backwards, Rick Fischer watched his comrades turn and rush past him. They were heading for a door that stood open at the back of the room. Rick took several steps back towards the creature that was now struggling to stand on the table. Opening his arms out wide, they could tell that he was trying to protect it from harm.

Now that Rick Fischer had lost his companions, a look of confusion and worry crossed his face. While he stood there, Toni Sillwood turned the talisman of Yggdrasill on end. She pointed it straight at the head of the creature, now standing precariously on the table. The nightmare creature's head was now visible over Rick's left shoulder. It was levitating into the air, rising above him in slow motion, as Mike Dean watched in awed silence. He saw an almost imperceptible beam of crackling light emitting from the talisman. The light hit the obscene figure square between the eyes. Rearing up into the air, the creature howled in agony. After thrashing around wildly it imploded, with an earth-shattering burst of raw energy. The sound rocked the building to its foundations, causing cracks to appear in the walls. The noise assaulted Mike's ears, threatening to burst his eardrums. As the pressure wave washed over the group, it caused them all to crouch down in pain.

When he'd recovered enough to be able to open his eyes again, Mike Dean looked across the room. Through streaming eyes, he saw that Rick Fischer had drawn a revolver from under his thick black gown. Within a few split seconds, before Mike could raise the alarm, he fired off three rounds. He had taken direct aim at Toni Sillwood, but she didn't flinch. She stared straight back at Rick, fixing him with her fierce glare as if she was daring him to try again. With the talisman in her hands now turned lengthways, the bullets stopped in mid-air. They had been fired from a few feet away and couldn't have missed, but they dropped impotently to the floor. The bullets bounced off the stone slabs before coming to rest at Toni's feet.

With a look of disgust, Toni Sillwood turned the talisman on end once again. This time she was pointing it directly at Rick Fischer. They all watched the faint stream of light as it reached across the room and washed over him. For a few moments Rick Fisher looked as if he was having trouble controlling his fingers. His eyes dropped to his hands in amazement as he let go of the revolver and watched it fall to the ground. Seconds later he collapsed to the floor himself. After laying there thrashing about for a few moments, he curled up into a tight ball. By the time that Mike reached him, he was jabbering furiously. When he placed his hand on Rick's shoulder, he gave off an insane cry, like someone who had lost their mind.

With its work done, the talisman stopped emitting its beam of light. The whole atmosphere of the room changed as the talismans' power died. The aura of intense evil that had been flowing through the basement, evaporated away in moments. Left behind was a fresh, light feeling, like a spring morning. Walking to the back of the room, where she had put the flightcase, Toni Sillwood repacked the talisman. As she locked it away in its case, Mike Dean searched around for a light switch. The room exploded with bright fluorescent illumination from the overhead lighting when Mike hit the button. It revealed the horror of the room in stark intensity.

Mike Dean stepped back over to where Rick Fischer was laying. As he drew near to the man, he scampered away into a dark corner behind the table. He was still jabbering incoherently, his eyes flicking about but seeing nothing. It looked as if his mind had overloaded and that some circuit deep inside had blown. Under the bright overhead lights, the room appeared plain and shabby. The black cloth that covered the table hung in tatters, the plaster on the walls was crumbling and cracked. There was now little to show of the horror that had played out before them, other than a thick layer of gritty grey dust. It spread over the end of the room where the table stood, where the creature had been sitting.

Leaving the basement, Mike Dean followed Toni Sillwood back up the stairs. They made their way along the deserted hallway in silence, neither of them knowing what to say. Trying several of the doors that they passed, they found rooms that were all empty. There was nothing of interest to uncover. In the end they came across a small office at the front of the building, close to the main door. It was the first room they had found that showed any sign of occupation.

The walls were hung with photographs of Rick Fischer alongside a mixture of other people. In all the pictures the regulation armbands were the main focus of attention. Pride of place on the wall opposite the door was an enormous portrait of Rick Fischer, he was standing in front of an ornate pentagram. Ignoring the pictures, Toni walked across the room towards a large desk. Grabbing the phone that was sitting there, she checked that it was working before punching in a stream of numbers. A few moments later, she spoke some words in German and replaced it into its cradle.

Several minutes later, Tac joined them in the office. They were glancing through a pile of right-wing propaganda and other papers that sat in open boxes on the floor, when the front door of the building burst open. Four men launched themselves into the passage, in an almost militaristic manoeuvre. Rushing out of the office, Toni Sillwood spoke a few words of a language that sounded ancient. She held out a silver disc towards the men, who stared at it. Looking at the disc, the man at front of the group nodded and said something in the same language. He relaxed a little after the tense mode of his arrival. Toni ran through the events that they had witnessed since entering the house. Once she had finished, the man told her that it would be best for them to leave the area as soon as possible. There was nothing more for them to do.

Mike Dean mentioned that Rick Fischer was still in the basement room. He was in a bad way, but the men said that they would take care of him. They would cleanse the area to make sure that there were no traces of what had happened there. Leaving the building, they headed back towards the car. On the way, Toni Sillwood explained that the men were part of the German group she had spent so long trying to find. They were closely aligned to the Union of the Mountain Ash. She had been attempting to make contact with someone from the group since their arrival in Germany. The group had been drawn towards her after her first use of the talisman. They were able to sense the infinite power that it unleashed. The talisman had acted like a beacon to them, drawing them to her.

Happy to take to the wheel, when they reached the car, Mike Dean drove back to the hotel. Once there, they packed their bags and checked out. Now the whole affair was over, they all wanted to make it to Hannover as soon as possible. Richard and the girls would be waiting for them, and they would be wondering what had gone on.

# With Thanks

For her belief and encouragement, I would like to thank my daughter, Jess.

A special mention also has to go to my mum, Peggy Eaton, who was always encouraging and will be missed by us all.

# A Message from the Author

Music has always been a massive part of my life, having worked in the business for many years. There have been many albums playing while I've been sitting at the computer, writing. I'm not one for playlists though, sorry Jess, but here are just a few of the albums that were played regularly.

Jaz Coleman – Magna Invocatio

Aphrodite's Child – 666

Apocalypse Orchestra – The End is Nigh

Killing Joke – Pandemonium

New Model Army – From Here

Scott Walker – Soused

Anna Calvi – Hunter

Doctors of Madness – Dark Times

Printed in Poland
by Amazon Fulfillment
Poland Sp. z o.o., Wrocław

65072018R00129